AF415305

WWW.INDEPENDENTLEGIONS.COM

Kyla Lee Ward

Those That Pursue Us Yet

Novella

ISBN: 979-12-80713-79-7
December 2023

Copyright (Edition) ©2023 Independent Legions Publishing
Copyright (Work) ©2023 Kyla Lee Ward
Cover Art: Alessandro Amoruso
Copyediting: Karen Runge
All Rights Reserved

RECIPIENT OF HWA SPECIALTY PRESS AWARD

For David

Some fears belong to childhood,
Phantasms we forget,
But nothing can be stronger than,
Those that pursue us yet.

And Wander dreams.

The streets she traverses may be cracked and potholed, with graffiti in dead languages, future languages and languages that have never existed caking the windowless walls. They may undulate with cobblestones, shadowed by gables and brooding shapes that clutch and caw. The simoon sifts red sand over the faint tracks she left wandering through the columns of a ruined temple. But here, in this facsimile of the branch office where she works during the day, she is surrounded by figments resembling her workmates. Fingers crook over keyboards and touch pads, eyes are glued to screens.

Threading through them, she recognises the first sign. Phobetor has found her trail, and It is closing in.

After all these years, she knows how It affects the dreamscape, even when still at a distance. Something like a chime alerts her, well before the tell-tale patterns of decay, of weight and thickening intrude upon her own imagery. Once, It would only manifest in deep dreams, beyond the border, but more and more of late It is entering the shallows where mere memories lie, among the mundane reflections of home and work. And so she hastens now towards waking.

The dream-office matches the real in every detail, and she knows her way to the fire door and the back exit. She crosses the open expanse of parquet flooring, workspaces only partially concealed by partitions of frosted glass. But the fans are soundless and no one hails her; there is none of the soft murmur of telephone calls and discussion that permeates the place in reality. And now she sees that the occupants of those cubicles are blackened corpses. Their scalps are soft with the ash of burned hair, their eyes boiled in their sockets, limbs twisted into postures of agony. Ichor pools on the floor, emitting not a true scent but the threat of one, causing her to instinctively recoil. Around her, the clean, metal curves of the furniture are beginning to decline, to soften. The air shimmers wetly.

This is bad. She is near to waking now, near to her body, and this is very, very bad.

How did It get this close without her realising? It usually takes longer than this for It to pick up the trail after she changes city, but even then, she's had the signs to warn her. There is only one answer that she can see: It must have followed her to Paris, then lain low *deliberately*—but these are thoughts for after she's woken. She needs a way out, now, but not to her bed, the studio and her life. She must dive back into the deep dream and lose It before waking by a different route.

Jumping dreams is her best option. It is not always possible, but nonetheless she makes the attempt. The trick is to find something within the *mise-en-scène* which by association can lead her elsewhere—from the office to, let's say, a phantasm of the Charles de Gaulle airport? A nexus of transport is always a good choice: lots of figments, lots of motion. And from there, she might go any place at all.

She concentrates. Summons her memories and desires.

The glass of the cubicle morphs into a sliding panel topped with a security camera—beyond it, she sees a vast expanse, airplanes dipping and gliding like colourful fish in a giant aquarium. But attached to the door is a tiny metal name plate reading "Branch

Manager, Princess Perdita". It is not her name and yet it is, at the same time.

She pulls up sharply. She may have grown careless this past year, but she knows a trap when she sees it.

As she pauses, a shadow falls over the expanse of the airport and ragged shapes curl and weave beyond the glass.

Grasping for imagery gone fluid yet heavy, as thick and sticky as tar, she wills herself to rise. This is a blunt manoeuvre: eschew the planes, simply punch through the office ceiling and fly as far and fast as she can, under her own power. Soaring over the rooftops, she may see the streets of the City of Lights winding beneath her like dead coral in a lagoon. But although she leaves the floor, the ceiling comes no closer. She feels herself beginning to drag, as though weights are attached to her feet.

All that her strongest willing can achieve is that she turn away from the door she visualised, that It had *anticipated* she would visualise, and bound away in giant, clumsy leaps back towards the office entrance. On hands as feet she gambols, the inertia dragging her sense of self into something long and leonine. As the parquet blackens beneath her. As the space between her and the office door stretches and becomes an ever-steepening slope. It is like trying to run up a wave.

Ambushed, she still has a few tricks.

She concentrates. Summons a very specific image that she has practised with before. Not a literal door this time: her new visual is a square of concrete pavement, bathed in the sun of late afternoon. So intense is her imagining, so accurate, she can see the cracks sneaking across it, sprouting tiny leaves. The top-right corner hosts the imprint of an autumn long-ago, when the concrete was fresh. A single sycamore leaf with curled edges is reproduced exactly in the medium: those green intruders will have seeded and died a million times before it fades. She envisages the leaf; she envisages the paving as if it lies at the bottom of the office stairwell. The stairwell that lies at the top of the slope of blackened parquet, now curling in on her like a wave about to break.

The drag on her ceases: she hurtles elastically through the murk. Why has It stopped pulling? Because It knows; It feels that she is moving closer. The step towards her body is one she is permitted to take.

Cresting the wave, she sees the office stairwell from the full height of the top floor; a concrete cylinder with steel steps spiralling down and down around a void. But simultaneously, she feels the heat bouncing back up from the concrete. Hears the sound of the traffic on their street and the laughter of children. And she lets herself fall.

The momentum of her release drives her towards the concrete eight floors down. The unending, unclimbable slope may be one of the basic gambits of nightmare, but so too is falling.

And Wander wakes.

***

She woke at the moment of impact, the precise moment her dream form slammed against the concrete. Another instinctive reaction, only this time the suggested shock triggered a *physical* reflex. Her own muscles woke her. It was a good trick; only possible in the shallows. She woke in her bed, the studio, her life, jarred prematurely out of sleep and leaving Phobetor behind. But not far behind. Not far away at all.

Heavy. She always felt so heavy upon waking: nonetheless, she moved. Cold sweat drenched the sheets dragging after her like rags, like bandages, as she rolled over the side of the bed. It was a large bed, even when shared by her and the man who now roused, grumbling. It was set very close to the floor. The sheets were red, as deep as blood, and there were rings set into the headboard of black wrought iron. They had their uses. All the supple leather and rubber things upon the bedside table had their uses. Here, she felt safe.

"Chrissalfuckinmighty." Roscoe emerged from the sheets, all ribs and muscle, bronze in the light that splintered in purples and amber through the scarf hung across the window. They were discrete in their games, in this neighbourhood of children, sun, and old pavement. "Wander, what's wrong?"

Her heart thrummed like a hummingbird's, she burnt and froze, all at once. Her hair stuck to her back as sweat trickled down her spine, her own scent drowned in patchouli and black peony.

"I think we have to move again." There, she'd said it. No excuses, no dodging the truth, even though she knew what would come now.

"We've only been here a year and a half! For fuck's sake!" But then he lowered his voice, smoothed it to pleading with a Californian burr. "Just tell me what it is. What it *really* is this time. Please?"

Slowly, she peeled the linen from her skin. Let it drop around her as her heart calmed, as her temperature slowly stabilised. At long, long last she told him. "Because Phobetor has found me."

∗∗∗

And Wander remembers.

Twenty-eight years is a long time ago; at least, as humans measure time. To a child, it is unimaginable. She could never have dreamt of Paris, this ten-year-old girl with pale skin and dark hair webbing the pillow, lying so still in her hospital bed. White the room, so white, like the heart of a cloud. But this cloud is seeded with machines.

They surround the bed: wires and one long, clear tube connecting the dials and displays to appropriate parts of the little body. They are not her only companions: somehow, a woman has found a niche in which to sit. She has golden hair, this woman, greying at the edges as if singed, and rich, peachy skin. Even granted the softening and sharpening of age, her face and the girl's are nothing alike. But deep worry is etched around her drooping eyes. Even in her doze, she keeps a hand on the bed.

Until the steady beeping of the machines suddenly increases in pace.

Until the woman jerks and opens bloodshot, blue eyes as the shadows of nurse and doctor appear on the curtain.

Until the girl's eyes open, pale green and unknowing.

"She's awake! Honey, honey, can you hear me?"

Wander hears her. She hears all the commotion and sees the activity around her, without context. Why is she suddenly so heavy? What is this smell and this pain? And what is this thing she feels in her mouth, in her throat...?

Her whole body contorts as she finds her answer, and she screams, then gags on the tube. Hands fall on her: she thrashes, attempting to push them off, to yank out the impediment and keep on running...

"Wander, Wander it's all right! I'm here! Someone call Phillip at the house!"

Then at all once, she realises she is awake. But this isn't her bedroom, which she shares with her little sister. Her mother is here but that man in white is not her father. Where is she and why are they holding her down?

Her dream had started in the house, as usual. It had been a summer's night in Sydney, full of chirping, clicking and heat. She remembers that. It is easier for many people to remember from waking to waking than to retain the content of an intervening dream. But Wander does. She always remembers.

Wasn't it common to dream, initially, of your own bedroom smouldering in charcoal and umber, with a full moon forcing its gaze through the cracks? Reli was sleeping, not dreaming, in her bed on the other side of the room; a little pile of golden curls emerging from a whorl of sheet. It is a fact of their family that Reli resembles their mother through and through. Their father has red hair, so Wander's lack of colour is presumed to be a throwback to some distant ancestor.

In her dream, Wander had exited the bedroom, walking with exaggerated concentration through the darkened house—if she didn't concentrate, her feet would leave the floor and she wouldn't be able to control where she was going. The contents of the living room glinted like half-buried gems, all their parents' precious souvenirs from Bali and Tibet, and the low table where her mother liked to work. Even in a dream, she could not enter; a daytime forbiddance manifesting as a wall of solid glass. The same impediment barred her from their parents' bedroom and her father's study: thick ice, unmelting, encasing computer and books. Growing bored with this, she sought the back door. It was then that she heard Reli calling.

For a moment, she paused on the back step. Then resentment flared in her and she made her escape. Being a big sister took up enough of her time in the day.

She could wander out into a dream of the suburb where they lived. The streets, the shops and park were mostly empty, but sometimes she encountered figments of the people who belonged there. If she mentioned this to them in waking, the response was usually smiles and laughter, oh-how-sweet, but sometimes they stared at her oddly. In any case, such things would not satisfy her tonight.

The forest loomed at the very back of their back yard, past the swing-set that Reli still used but which she was too big for, and the overgrown vegetable patch. Beyond the fence of ragged, grey palings, all was night-blind acacia and undulations of eucalyptus, cascading with moonlight. The forest was different from the suburb: the fence, she somehow knew, was more than a fence. Once she passed through, the replicas of daylight things would fall away and she could go anywhere. Wind through the trees on glow-worm lit paths, passing witch-cottages and goblin-caverns, to the garden where the plants all moved. If she wished, she could continue onward to the city with its mansions and marvels, beyond which lay the great, red desert. The figments she encountered there were different, and some were not people at all.

She jumped the fence and her feet left the ground. She flew far into the trees, that night; very far indeed.

Maybe too far.

"Oh Wander, please look at me! That's right. Do you know me?"

Wander always remembers her dreams. But this time, she finds it hard. The further she goes, beyond the mountains to the plains beyond, it is harder to describe or draw anything that she sees, once she wakes. And this time...

A vast chasm with stairs leads through an archway to a colonnade to a courtyard glinting with fountains and twined with crimson flowers, to parades of sphinxes and vast statues like people upholding tree-lined avenues. Stars that may be glints of water cling to the moss on the side of a giant tree. Or is the tree a mere sapling, sprouting from the cracks in the marble below the sculpted railing on which she leans? She cannot tell. And through the archway lie other archways, the stairs lead to other stairs, the courtyards to other courtyards, and she is searching, for what she cannot tell. But it seems she knew this place at some past time and recognises this, even though the layout has changed. Everything about it has changed.

She was lost there, she thinks. Maybe for a long time.

A place where something had fallen. Space junk, shell casing or feather. A ring of destruction, of shattered columns, slivered weapons and broken toys surrounding a sleek and lightless Something that twitches like a freshly severed limb.

And then she had found... no. She had *been* found.

She shivers through her entire body and the doctor descends with devices. Wander's skin is clammy cold and still she does not speak. She is not nearly ready to speak.

Frightening things dwell in the forest and the desert holds its share of peril. Not even the garden is completely safe. When she drew a picture, in crayon, of the walking sunflowers with all their teeth, her teacher in class 2W had been very concerned. That time she told Reli about the sharks with legs that emerged from the sand. Reli had been scared and their mother got angry with her. But *this* had been different.

And It had seen her, for just a moment.

Only she was faster, so much smaller and faster than It. She escaped and ran all the way home. Which this isn't. She's confused and upset.

"Please Wander. Say something!"

She gazes into her mother's haunted eyes and her tongue twitches. "I... I had a bad dream."

She has been comatose for five full days.

In time, she will learn to be more careful when she passes beyond the fence. In time, she will learn that it is already too late.

But here inside the cloud (that stinks of cleaning fluid and vomit), she is promised ice cream if she leaves the sticky things on her head, if she lets the doctor prick her arm and draw her blood. She does not like this but nods her head, aware that if she resists, it will only take longer. And already, at age ten, she knows that if she tells them what she remembers of her dream, they will make her stay here.

As the doctors work around her, she focuses on the one, crucial thing. She doesn't know if she really heard Reli calling her or not. Reli appears sometimes in the dream-house, happy to talk to her sister and follow her about. Sometimes, when she was a little younger, she would mention it to Wander the next day as if it were all perfectly normal.

Reli is the only person ever to do that.

Reli can never be allowed to follow her over the fence. That terrible darkness must never find her sister.

The next thing she says to her mother is, "I want my own room."

***

PARIS, 2012

It was Friday afternoon, at fourteen hundred hours precisely. In the last weeks of summer, central Paris was still as hot and humid as July.

Dr Madeline Diomande smiled and consulted a still-largely blank form while studying her new patient. Her consulting room, on the sixth floor of the medical centre in Saint-Sulpice, was bright and open, with potted orchids in the window and mint-green walls. The chairs and rug exploded with colour, to echo the glorious wax-printed *pagnes*, which were her grandmother's and which she had framed on the wall. It was always instructive to see whether a person expanded into this space or shrank from it, whether they contrasted or blended. Dressed in black, with an old, leather jacket draped across her shoulders, this woman almost dissolved.

"So, Wanda Paxton. How may I help you today?" She said this in English. Although the woman had greeted her in excellent French, English was listed as her first language. She had been referred by her workplace health fund; said workplace being a multinational insurance company with a local branch.

"It's Wander. E-R." The correction was automatic, neither hostile nor defensive. "If you think that's bad, my sister got Realise."

Madeline made a surreptitious notation. "A sister. Are you the eldest, or—"

"Eldest. They're all back in Australia."

The form revealed that Wander was thirty-eight years old—the same age as Madeline herself. Otherwise, they could not have been more different. Wander's hair was dark and drifted softly around a pale face, drawn and shadowed with sleeplessness. Madeline's skin was deep and gleaming, her hair perfectly moisturised and raked into an elegant cone, and of course, *she* was the one behind the desk.

Already suspecting the answer, Madeline repeated her question. "How may I help you, Wander?"

"I'm here at my partner's suggestion. He thinks... I don't know what he thinks." Wander knotted her fingers in her lap. "Look, I'm having these nightmares. I have for a long time, but recently, they've been getting worse."

Madeline listened as Wander (parents aspirational, doubtless pushy) described an anxiety scenario so classic as to rouse her suspicions.

"And this Phobetor, whatever it may be, is associated with your work?" The name is familiar, Madeline thinks; likely from mythology.

"It found me there, but that's not—it's not my job that's worrying me. I like my job."

"It says here that you're a claims assessor, specialising in commercial properties." There were four languages and two degrees listed on Wander's form; a BA in Communications from the University of Sydney and a BSc in Forensic Science undertaken at Berkeley, partly by correspondence. She had found a novel way to utilise them, Madeline thought. "Have you been in Paris long?"

"A year and a half. I move around, you see, from branch to branch. I've lived in Sydney, Brisbane, Singapore; ah, those six months in San Francisco probably count. Guangzhou, Los Angeles and Budapest."

"A true *citizen du monde*." Madeline kept her voice gentle. "But Phobetor follows you? No matter where you go?"

"Yes, and it's..." Long, pale fingers, knotting and unknotting. "You know how sometimes you dream about places you know in the real world?"

"Yes, of course. All dream imagery ultimately derives from waking experience."

"How..." Knotting and unknotting. "What does it mean if something like *It* appears in a place, in a dream, that's really close to where you actually are?"

"I would suggest," said Madeline, still gentle, "in very general terms, that it means you can no longer ignore whatever it is that the image represents."

A slight flush crossed the pallid cheeks. "It's not that simple."

"Oh no, far from it. For a start, there are two important factors here. The recurring nightmare of the entity that pursues you and the fact that, after eighteen months, you are dreaming of Paris."

"Why wouldn't I dream of Paris?"

"The places we dream about are places that mean something to us; to which we attach a strong emotion. Dreams of returning to your childhood home, for instance."

"I don't dream of my childhood home. In case Reli..."

When the sentence remained unfinished, Madeline said, "It's all right, Wander, you can speak or not. But you should know that this is a safe place. Nothing you say here will ever leave it. Now, who is Phobetor?"

Wander shrugged. "The Roman god of nightmares. I don't know if that's what It actually is, but that is the closest description I've ever found."

"What does it look like?"

"*In the form of beast or bird or the long serpent.*" Dark waves fell across Wander's face, as she bent her head. "That's Ovid, the *Metamorphoses.*"

Madeline's skin prickled. There *was* something real here; something that this woman had repressed and which was now pushing towards her conscious mind through the natural and vital channel of dreams. Given the way Wander had dismissed her childhood, Madeline knew where the problem was rooted, and she could guess as to its nature. But the psychiatrist does not construct the narrative. That is the patient's work, which she must do, if not alone. The terror that only she can face, no matter how ingeniously she has displaced it.

Madeline smiled again, this time with real sympathy. "It's all right. We don't need to discuss that now. How about you tell me about your sister? Do you keep in touch?"

"All right." Under the hair, Wander seemed to be bracing herself. "All right, I'll do this if you tell me what you think of the idea that dreams are... real within themselves. That they have their own existence and things that happen there can affect *us?*"

And Madeline understood, suddenly, how Wander's anxiety had influenced her entire life. That she had *literally* fled this nightmare around the globe. It was astounding. She understood too, that if she didn't reassure Wander that her concerns were not trivial, the woman would never trust her.

Universals would not do here.

"When I was a student," Madeline said slowly, selecting her words. "I would sometimes unravel problems in my sleep. Work my tutor had set. I'd write essays in my dreams and then use them when I woke."

Wander hadn't moved, but she was listening. Every line of her hunched posture said she was hanging on Madeline's words. She needed to give Wander more.

"Sometimes... if I'm tired or anxious when I go to sleep, sometimes I'll be dreaming about that. Then I... no matter where my dream was located to start with, I'll find myself on the beach. A beach my family used to holiday at when I was growing up. It was beautiful."

Wander's face reappeared; a single, greenish eye. "It's very bright in here," she said. "Would you mind if I closed the shutters on the window?"

Madeline did not mind. They discussed Wander's family, her job (which Madeline was sure was contributing to her stress) and her current relationship, with an artist who had followed her from Los Angeles. At the close of session (promptly at fifteen-fifteen), Wander booked the same slot for the next six weeks.

***

And Madeline remembers.
Twenty-eight years is an inconceivable time. The other side of the world is an inconceivable place, and if the ten-year-old girl playing on the beach at Toulon ever thinks of Australia, it is as a myth no different to Avalon or El Dorado. A girl with deep and gleaming skin, her hair like dense smoke.

The beach is beautiful, yes. But during these childhood summers, it is a rare day that she does not succumb to the compulsion to dare the littoral; dodging the crash and spread of the waves. The rules are fixed—the damp sand can only be entered once the water itself retreats, leaving a pristine and polished surface. She herself must retreat at the last possible moment before the wave returns. Her mother sits on the dry sand, draped in bright cotton and a broad-brimmed hat, smiling at her daughter's antics, never guessing that at a single misplaced step, the clasp of so much as an inch of water around a tiny ankle could see her child dragged out of sight.

There is no logic to this game, no cause beyond the girl's internalisation of some infantile Thou Shalt Not. If her mother should join her, in her coral bikini, if her brother or father accompanies her into the water, she will splash and laugh, even swim. She glances up the beach, where the men of her family stand knee-deep in turquoise. Antoine is shouting something; the roll and crash take the words, but they are directed at their father. Papa looks serious, anxious, but she cannot see Antoine's face. She thinks she might join them, and they'll go for sugar doughnuts at the café in the old town. But first, she must face one more wave.

Madeline lets her gaze drop to the settling sand, stepping into the danger zone. A cold seepage surrounds her feet. The wave has left tiny shells and pebbles in their own, watery depressions. Some of these were there before the water covered them: how can that be? Perhaps they are not pebbles at all. If she tried to pick them up, would she find they were the tiniest tip of something deep below, reaching towards the light?

It is the noise that alerts her, the rolling, boiling sound of a wave already broken and headed straight towards her. Scything glass seeks her toes. She jumps away but has failed to see a secondary wash peeling towards her from the opposite direction: a wild leap saves her but landing, she staggers. For a moment, she offers not just ankle but her entire body to the water's grip—teetering between life and death, until the wave recedes.

Now her feet are caked in hot, bright sand. Her mother is near. She turns back to the sparkling sea and glimpses her brother's long, brown back as he is dragged out into the surf.

She screams.

He is fine, that day. He was bodysurfing, not drowning, and his argument with their father was about a movie. But the time would come, yes—and soon—when Antoine would pull on a black beret and vanish into the night.

Her parents' marriage did not survive it. She and her mother stayed in Paris while her father went to Abidjan, to look after the business.

It's decades later now, and she knows, intellectually, that Antoine is dead. She also knows that the forces which took him, the hatred, intolerance and fear, are once again surging in Paris.

Antoine did not drown, but she can only think of him in terms of crashing waves.

***

And Madeline wakes.

She shivered in her night gown, despite the warmth of her lover curling at her back. Her dream was now nothing more than fragments and terror. Staring into the cluttered darkness of their bedroom, she was convinced for a moment that vast waves were lapping at the door. That if she were to open the shutters and gaze out from the tiny balcony of their apartment, she would see not the crumbling brick back-streets of Montrouge, but the ocean heaving under starlight.

She slipped on her robe of floral silk and stood in bare feet on the old floorboards. Back under the duvet, Giselle sighed and stirred, but only briefly. Madeline did not go to the shutters: instead, she slipped noiselessly into the kitchenette, where she sat on a stool in the dark and listened to the cracks and creaks, as the old apartment block slowly cooled. She heard the drone of the elevator and the rattling of pipes in the walls, but little from outside.

Giselle was a journalist on the political desk of *Le Monde*, currently running herself ragged on the campaign trail. The election was still months away, but she brought home dire warnings on an almost daily basis; sometimes breathless reports of flung bottles and Nazi slogans. Here beyond the boulevard Périphérique all was passably quiet, but nonetheless, Madeline wondered what she would do if she heard gunfire approaching. If she found hate speech painted on their door.

In familiar shadows, Madeline reached for *tisane* and her favourite mug. As the kettle boiled, her thoughts shifted to dark hair and pale green eyes, a slightly bitten lip. This was unusual; she had long since mastered the art of leaving her work back in Saint-Sulpice. Perhaps it was the confidence she'd shared, about the dream of the beach, though she had not told her patient its real meaning.

As the boiling water released the fragrance of mint and lemon balm, Madeline admitted it to herself: after one session, Wander Paxton had engaged her in a way that most of her patients never did. Such an interesting woman, such a wonderful child she must have been; the joy of her pretentious, pushy parents, and yet so vulnerable. Imprintable, as children are, with appalling fear. To all appearances, she had broken the pattern of abuse that so many victims keep repeating their whole lives (they would have to investigate her relationship with the artist, but she wasn't picking up that vibe). But she still suffered a compulsion to stay physically ahead of her psychic terror.

Perhaps this case could form the basis of a paper or at least a proposal. She had already been considering a return to study: grumbly old Legrange, who supervised her thesis, saw specialisation as a natural development for a psychiatrist. Perhaps, as she helped Wander Paxton, it would help her find her own way.

Madeleine sat in the darkness, contemplating the future and breathing in the rhythm of waves.

***

The following Friday, around fourteen-thirty.

Madeline spread her hands, empty for the moment of paper or pen. "What you describe is simply lucid dreaming. Not everybody does it, but it's not uncommon."

"Even if you can make changes to your dream, can change from one dream to another at will?"

"Lots of people report that too." She smiled. "Just as they report nightmares that take place in their office or bedroom and feel very real. These can be very disturbing. But as I told you at our first session, dreams come from waking. I assure you, Wander, there can be nothing in them you didn't encounter waking at some point, even if you don't remember."

"I'm quite sure I've never encountered a shark with legs," said Wander, "even in Australia."

"I'm quite sure you were taken to the beach at a young age," Madeline replied. "Perhaps there were strangers there and you were told not to go near them. Perhaps, in your dream, you conflated two dangers into one very effective symbol. Dreams work through symbols, as I'm sure you're aware."

"Anyway," Wander continued, "It's not that I see sharks with legs; it's that when I see them, I can fly away. Or I can create a door to somewhere safer, closer to the shallows."

"The shallows?"

"You know, the dreams of your work and all the everyday things. The dream of your bedroom, just before you wake up."

Madeline leant forward in her chair. "I can say with some confidence that I do not always dream of my bedroom at either end of the night. Perhaps you are recalling a hypnagogic, pre-sleep state."

"Perhaps." Wander also leant forward. "Anyway, it's not until you pass through all that, till you cross the border into the deep, that things get interesting."

"The border?"

"Somewhere in the dream. You'll have your own somewhere." Wander looked straight at her, challenging her to deny it.

"And you have to pass this border," Madeline said, "And travel back through the ordinary dreams, to your bedroom, in order to wake?"

"Yes!"

"Are you aware," said Madeline, retrieving her pen, "how perfectly you have just described the stages of sleep? How the brain slows from alpha down to delta waves before entering REM sleep, and then speeds back up towards waking?"

Wander's face fell. "You're not listening to me."

"I am and it is very interesting. But the fact remains that none of these things you do are helping you evade Phobetor. Not anymore."

"That's true." Wander slumped, shoulders twitching.

"So, what do you think? Why has it suddenly got so close?"

Wander's hair closed over her face. "I got careless I suppose."

"How have you liked living in Paris? Have you encountered any stressful situations with the transition?"

Wander shook her head, then muttered. "I do like it here. Roscoe likes it too. It's good for his painting, as you'd imagine."

"Do you think you might like to stay?"

"I've never really considered settling down anywhere."

"But you have a partner now who seems quite determined to stick around. And there's a sign on the road ahead, saying forty—slow down?"

"You think that's why It's getting closer? Because I'm thinking of settling down?"

Madeline flicked the idea into a minty corner. "Just something to consider, perhaps, while we try and build a better picture of this *chimera*."

They had established that Phobetor wielded decay-imagery and beast-imagery that *intruded* into Wander's dreams. She had no awareness that she, ultimately, was the source of this. It was an amorphous, shifting shape like a dark fog, although the closer It came, the more It coalesced into a discrete figure, like someone wearing a heavy cloak with tattered edges. Wander insisted she knew no more. She had never allowed It to get nearer.

She never *allowed* It—again, Madeline noted the choice of words. "Are you aware of the legend of the mare? We call such dreams nightmares, but originally the mare was believed to be a creature, a demon that attacked sleepers in their beds. Other cultures called it an *alp*, or a *lamashtu*, but all—"

"It's not like that! Phobetor is a child of Somnus and brother to Morpheus, and controls all nightmares."

"What does It want? Tell me exactly what you think will happen if It trails you all the way back to your bedroom."

Wander was silent for a long, long minute. Then her lip twisted. "When I was a child, I slipped into a coma for five days. They never found a reason despite years, *years* of tests."

"That's dreadful," said Madeline, as all her assumptions about the case suddenly spun on this new axis—which she *should* have unearthed during their first session. "It's a horrible thing for a child, to be so ill."

"I wasn't ill, that's the point," said Wander, staring down at the floor.

Madeline had seen all the indicators of abuse in Wander—she still did. But this was a wildcard. "What do you remember about that time?"

"Everyone looking at me like I'd done something wrong. I'd upset everything."

"Children are very sensitive to that kind of thing. Even when the parents don't mean it, their disquiet creates an impression that can be very hard to get over."

"But that wasn't why..." Wander bit her lip, then raised her head. "All right then, *yes*. That is what I'm afraid of: that it will happen again, only this time, I'll never wake." Her eyes had been challenging, but now their focus slipped inward, to something only Wander could see. "It won't let me get away again."

Madeline could tell they would get no further today.

Still, progress had been made. She smiled and led the conversation back to Wander's work as a claims assessor. Wander seemed happy enough to share tales of arson and negligence, and her recent discovery of subsidence in the cellar of a wine bar on the Boulevard Raspail. This was followed by a ghastly tale about American mould. But if her work was the source of the decay motif in her nightmares, Wander did not recognise that either. At fifteen-fifteen, Madeline asked if Wander was returning to her workplace for the remainder of the afternoon, but apparently a flexi-day had been arranged. Roscoe was waiting to take her home.

As Wander laid her hand upon the doorknob to exit, Madeline saw her pause. She observed, then, a patient's ritual. Wander pulled the door to in front of her, as if blocking her own escape, then closed her eyes. Blindly, she opened it again to walk through. Madeline might have queried this, only they had run slightly over time and she had to prepare for Monsieur Bernard.

***

"I think I went too far today." Hovering on her own doorstep, Wander knew she was taut, as strung as she might be from hooks and straps. "I told the doctor things about dreaming, how it *works*."

Roscoe shut the front door, sealing off the outside world. Inside the studio, everything was as they would have it. "What does that matter, darling, when she won't believe a single word you say?"

"That's true," said Wander, but the sense of panic, of a guard dropped, remained. "She came back with all this stuff about brainwaves and asked about my job. I told her—" laughter choked her throat, "—I told her about a certain studio in Westho, how everyone who used it kept getting sick, but the owner refused to acknowledge there was a problem. Then, when I made him remove the panel, the solid mass of mould was nearly as large as the wall."

"An interesting choice." Roscoe walked over to the lounge and sat down.

Their studio was a warehouse conversion, all one large room with stairs leading up to a loft where Roscoe worked. Now all the space around them swam in shadow, pierced by the single beam of a reading lamp. The purple and amber veil across the window was blank now, waiting for the lamps to come on in the alley outside. Quivering, she wanted nothing more than to lie down on those crimson sheets and sleep. No, that was the last thing she wanted. Would this plan of theirs work? Were their precautions enough? What if It found the leaf on Its own? They should run, run….

"As I understand the plan," Roscoe spread a leanly-muscled arm along the top of the lounge. "If this is going to work, you have to *do* the therapy. There can't be any faking."

"I know." To cover her jitters, she was working off her shoes. "I know, it's just... I wasn't expecting her to get under my skin."

"Yeah, shrinks will do that." He leant back, spreading his legs slightly in his old, paint-spattered jeans. "I understand, it feels like you're losing control. But you've got to, don't you? Just a little, to get where you want to go. Don't you now? Come here."

Despite the hooks and straps, she went to him. The old boards were silky beneath her bare feet.

They were both consummate players, in their complementary ways. It was how they came together so quickly, after she arrived at the mould-afflicted studio to find the artist standing at the head of his fellow tenants and scowling like a pit bull. She hadn't expected it would last more than a couple of months and yet, here he was. Even though she'd told him.

"Tell me," he said as she straddled him. His long hands slid slowly along her arms. "How do you change things in your dreams?"

"Oh Roscoe, please. I've given you what I can, and I just spent the afternoon—"

His hands tightened on her wrists. "You question me? You deny me this?" She arched in his grip, as he whispered, "Safe word?"

"The usual," she hissed.

"What I want," he said, starting to pull now, extending the curve of her spine with an expert's surety, "is complete control."

"Practice. It will just take time." She didn't know *how* to teach him if concentration and visualisation didn't work. As an artist, surely, he would be good at such things. And then the thought occurred to her: if Roscoe could not do what she did, perhaps she did nothing. Perhaps she really was delusional.

In that moment, she saw herself as she must look from the doctor's side of the desk. Worse still, she saw the years of sleepless nights and days of terror, resorting to cutting and other abuses before she found her proper outlet. Fighting with her parents, then with friends and lovers, all the bridges burned in her conviction that this was the only way any of them could be safe. All for a child's nightmare.

In Roscoe's grip, she shivered, began collapsing.

"Stop that. Whatever this is, you stop. I need you strong," he said.

The pressure on her spine increased.

"I need you to stay the course. I need you—"

She tautened, re-establishing their balance.

"—to tell me."

Delusion or not, she could play the game. "Something smaller," she gasped, "just to start."

She described how she made a touchstone of the leaf printed in the paving outside. How she could leap to there from anywhere in the shallows. How Phobetor knew the leaf lay somewhere between dreaming and waking for her. This was an important part of the plan.

"A symbol," he said, just like Dr Diomande. "I know about symbols. I can paint something like that."

"Is painting like dreaming? I don't know." The tension in her back was almost pain—her sternum cracked, released, but Roscoe held her there. She felt the strain quivering in his own wrists and legs.

"Tell me how to reach the deep dream. Where is the border in Paris?"

"If you want to cross, you have to find your own." Her breath caught as his tremors increased. "Do you remember the Parc de Saint-Cloud? How we went there for the concert that evening?"

"I most surely do," he said. The stress eased slowly. "Poor little girl who'd never heard of the Hives."

"Well, if you remember what we did on the slope beneath the chestnuts, how far we went once it got the dark, then you'll know where my border has settled. Maybe yours is there too. Beyond it, you'll have experiences unlike anything you've ever known, but you have to make sure and come back. You have to be on this side to wake."

He chuckled, a marvellous sound. "Oh man, this is crazy. Crazy as this place you reckon you've found in the tunnels."

"*Something's* down there, the signs are all over the building. But," she sighed, feeling the warm burn wash through her arms. Feeling the knot still tight in her gut. "We should probably complete this stage this first."

"It doesn't matter how far I go, you're still flying out ahead of us, thinking up things. *Doing* these things." He leaned into her, face alight. "I can't see your dreamscape, not well enough to paint it. You'll have to help me get there."

Oh, how she craved these real sensations! The scent of oil paint as they kissed; the hot salt-sweet of his mouth and the grate of stubble. The quickening of nerves from one end of her body to the other.

"So I'll be a part of this painting?" she breathed into his mouth, "Amongst all the shapes and the words. What will you paint me as?"

"As a queen." He shifted his grip to keep her upright as he slowly spread his legs. "With flaming crown and wings of smoke."

This was foreplay. The hooks and straps came later.

*****

A week passed, then another, from the last weeks of summer into autumn. The sun set incrementally earlier and strange things were happening in Paris. The forthcoming election filled many eyes and ears; there were demonstrations and rallies. But one evening there was a panic in the Metro and unusual numbers of people went to their doctors, claiming recurring nightmares of something vast and dark.

*****

When Madeline arrived home that Friday (having spent a tiresome hour with Monsieur Bernard and an exhausting one with Madame Beauchêne), it was to an empty apartment. As hungry as she was, she waited in the kitchenette, reviewing her notes from Wander's session and looking up salient details on the net, which turned out to be a risky undertaking. Until Giselle finally burst in the door.

"You shouldn't be taking the Metro home," Giselle announced. "It's dangerous."

Her lover had beautiful brown eyes and creamy skin. Her soft, blonde hair curled about her neck. An appreciation of such women, Madeline reflected, was one part of her wild years that had stuck.

"Why dangerous, my darling?"

"There was a stampede today, at Montparnasse. Six people were hospitalised."

Montparnasse was on her route home: nearly the middle, in fact. Had she seen anything? Noticed anything unusual in the announcements and the surge of the crowd?

Those beautiful eyes were clouded with concern. "No one knows how it started. There've been reports someone was stabbed or pushed off the platform, but I can't confirm it. Just, someone started screaming, then everyone was running. People were knocked over and trampled, or crushed against the walls."

A textbook mass panic, thought Madeline. But she said, "That's terrible. Are you all right?"

"Yes, I'm fine. I was at the Palais Bourbon for a press conference."

"How did you get home?"

"A taxi, eventually." Giselle put down her satchel. "Come on, let's cook."

And cook they did. After four years together, their movements between the fridge and the stovetop, cupboards and counter, were so coordinated they felt like a dance. Giselle chopped vegetables while Madeline put on the rice and drained the beans. As Giselle sautéed, Madeline made the sauce with cream and herbs. Once the result was plated, Giselle produced the glasses as Madeline uncorked the wine.

"Did you know," Madeline said, pouring, "that the sense of threat induced by restraints and suspension creates a rush of endorphins, equivalent to an illegal high?"

"No, I can't say that I did. Where did you hear that?" Giselle swapped out her glass for Madeline's, then carried both over to the table.

"Just research."

Giselle sat down and looked at her earnestly across the food. "There *is* something happening out there, beyond all the usual election crud. I can feel it."

"It all comes down to fear," said Madeline. "Fear of strangers but also fear of intimacy. Not necessarily fear of pain."

Giselle pointed her fork. "Aha! You haven't heard a word I said: you're thinking about a patient!"

Madeline looked down at her plate. "There is a patient, yes."

"And he or she is a sadomasochist?"

"That's not the reason she's seeing me. I think it's how she's been handling her problems, up till now."

"Well, that sounds serious. How's it going?"

"It was going well." *But then I suggested that she contact her sister, and she practically attacked me.*

They ate for a while in silence. Madeline found herself once again going back over the afternoon's exchange. She understood, she said, that Wander felt the need to discipline herself, to control as much as possible in her life. Did she agree that this need could extend to her memories? Did it not make sense that she would use every means at her disposal to control what she feared?

She placed her fork down on the plate. "This stampede, Giselle. Ten to one, there was never any stabbing or pushing. People don't admit to what they truly fear and sometimes it's buried—it could have been a face or a shadow, or anything that triggered the first one who screamed. And after that, everyone saw something different."

Giselle's smile was tired. "That's what I love about you. You always think there are reasons, that even the strangest, stupidest things make sense and there's always something you can do."

"Don't you?"

"I try." Giselle was slumping now, the wine transmuting her agitation into exhaustion. "I tell you, it's getting hard."

What else happened today? Madeline thought. *What did you see out there?* She said, "And here I thought you loved my sense of humour and unique personal style."

"Actually, it's your ass." Madeline burst out laughing. "Definitely, ass." They were both laughing. "Just be careful, please."

Madeline reached out and took Giselle's hand. "I know that bad things happen, I do. I'll be careful, but I'm not going to take a taxi twice a day travelling between Montrouge and Saint-Sulpice."

For a moment it looked like, exhausted or not, Giselle was going to argue. Then she nodded and drained the last of her wine. "Mm, this patient, of yours. Does she like being tied up?"

"I believe that's something she and her partner do."

"And do they have a safe word, to stop it if things get too rough?"

"I'd imagine so."

They went to bed, but Giselle was tired and after a very little spanking and giggling, she fell sound asleep.

***

And Madeline dreams.

"You have to understand, Maddy." Antoine sits opposite her in the patient's chair, wearing the uniform of the Black Dragons. "Mum and Dad think that just 'cause we dangle crosses round our necks, we're accepted. We're not."

She reaches across the desk for a pen but can find nothing.

At eighteen years old, Antoine is handsome, with high cheekbones and a sculpted nose, his skin gleaming, his hair thick beneath the black beret. "There are people out there, like you and me, being bashed because of the colour of their skin. Others are suffering too; the Arabs are getting hit bad. They're being killed at night on the streets and the police won't do anything. They reckon *is* the attackers *are* the police."

She tries to speak, to tell him that even if this is the case, vigilantism is not the answer. Violence is not the answer, and he can rebel in other ways... nothing comes out of her mouth. She cannot even move her lips.

And now the light seems brighter, and she can feel the floor beneath her feet is starting to crumble, to slip away like sand.

"I have to go out, Maddy, it's like... it's war, that's what it is. What if they hurt Mama? What if they hurt you?"

Bad things happen, the more if you go seeking them! Stay home! She tries and tries, but even when the waves are so close that the walls of her office are shaking, she cannot make him hear.

***

You're very protective of your sister. When was the last time you talked together? Wander considered.

Reli's last email was only a month ago—not that she told the doctor *that*. Madeline Diomande, with her linen suits and perfect hair, would surely consider it strange that siblings communicated only over such distance and at such intervals, and she was damned if she was letting the doctor get under her guard again.

People who were there with you at the time may remember things differently to you. Sometimes just the presence of the familiar can jog our memories, even the ones we have restrained.

She knew the doctor thought she and Reli had been abused. The bare idea was ridiculous: freckled Phillip with his hemp shirts and painstaking gender neutrals, teaching her to programme. Laurie with her golden curls and insistence on being the change you want to see in the world. But those two had somehow produced a pale little girl with web-fine hair, who at age ten had passed beyond even the deep dream and stood amid utter devastation, the spore of something that could ruin symbols....

A child's nightmare. A child who had genuinely believed she and her sister could share the same dreams—and what would Madeline say about that?

She could ring Reli, if she was truly worried, and say, *Do you remember how you used to run around after me in dreams? Have you ever dreamed of a creature in a black, hooded robe with tattered edges that twitch and try to grasp you as It gets nearer? Only, what you see isn't the whole creature?*

I might be crazy, thought Wander, *but I'm not that crazy.*

All the same, now that she considered it, the doctor might have a point.

She turned to Roscoe, who was sketching something at the table in one of his big notebooks. "I want to try something tonight," she said. "Take a risk."

"Oh yes?"

"I'm going to enter the dream of one of my old houses. While I'm there, I'm going to try and remember more of what happened there."

He looked up from his sketchpad, frowning. *He doesn't understand*, she thought. *Even after all this.*

But then Roscoe said, "How risky?"

"I could attract Its attention," she said, feeling a rush of relief. "So I'm going to need you to stay awake while I sleep. Just for an hour or so."

***

And Wander dreams.

Wander sees the bedroom with its two, small beds. She sees charcoal and umber; moonlight thrusting through the cracks as though the house is a badly-caulked ship in danger of foundering once the shadows are saturated. In reality, the house would be different now. Completely different. Her sister hasn't lived there in decades. But still, she is relieved in the extreme there is no sign of her, not even the figment of a sleeping child.

She sits down on her old bed. Allows the recollection of textures, scratchy and saggy, to stir her. Remembers how in the morning, she would wake to the sound of her father juicing fresh oranges in the kitchen: the juicer was loud, and she could smell the crushed peel.

Was it normal to grow up in a house with a playset at the back and a patio at the front, in a leafy suburb where there were no gangs, guns or stray dogs? To go for bushwalks and ride an orange bike along the winding streets? This was all *good*, a very recipe for healthy, stable children. So why was she like this? Why had she felt, for as long as she could remember, that her parents had somehow been cheated, forced to accept a cuckoo that clucked strange things and lay in a hospital bed, not this little cradle but the starched, prickly bed where you splayed, restrained by tubes and wires…

And then, like discovering an old drawing, or a book falling open on a much-loved fairy tale, it all comes back.

And Wander remembers…

Courtyards leading to other *courtyards glinting with fountains and twined with crimson flowers, to parades of sphinxes and vast caryatids themselves upholding tree-lined avenues. Water purls past the trailing shawl of roots. Do the tiny pots of that noria truly feed a river so wide the bridges spanning it appear as silver wires? Or is the noria itself gigantic, forced into humbleness only by the cosmic banyan tree? Or are those merely silver wires, strung across a drainage ditch to frighten birds?*

Far above the infinite complexities rise the turrets, attenuated narwhal eminences and declines of nautilus, forms as pure and perfect as a soprano's voice. A golden light bathes that place, dawn on a planet newly coalesced, that has travelled for eternity to meet a living eye. Incredible, precious and so ancient as to grant that word meaning, it calls to her, aches in her and the terror it brings to her is too vast for her mind to contain: it lies in pieces, blackened and broken across the dreamscape in a trail of ruin…

She remembers what it was like to have huge, dark wings.

Then, as she gazes upon the feather, she feels It *moving deep below. Feels* It *like she might feel her bones growing.*

And she pauses, just an instant, before running.

She feels the heaviness in the air. Sees the shattered columns start to soften and sag. But she pauses, knowing but not understanding, terrified but at the same time yearning. Just for an instant, just a glimpse…

She pauses and It *sees her. It says,* "Child."

Conglomerations of bone burst out of her spine.

Wander jumps up from the tiny, tiny bed and flees into the hallway. Deep russets and purples stripe the floor. There on the wall is the link she used to get here: a mounted picture of small boats on a brown river. Every detail of prow and sail, the ripples of the water and even the clouds surrounding the moon are made of bamboo, slivered, pressed and inserted into the design like a fine parquet. Oh, she can go many places from here. And go she must, flee back to the studio where Roscoe waits beside her sleeping body, away from such madness as cannot possibly be real....

But then, she pauses. For the first time, she looks on her childhood home with adult eyes.

The hall runs behind her, past the door to her parents' bedroom and the converted walk-in that became her own. She spent her adolescence sleeping next to the laundry, had been able to feel the dryer going through the wall. This house is *small*, barely larger than the studio, and the door at the end, through which the moonlight falls... well, what's out there is a tenuous set of swings that would probably be banned these days, a couple of cabbages and a fence. The border lies here no longer. The living room is a treasury of dark jewels, barred to her by a forbiddance of solid glass, ice. It shatters at a touch and inside, everything is junk! Really, it's all the crappiest kind of tourist bait from Bali, Tibetan flags and a salt crystal lamp obtained from some homewares shop, and a coffee table with brass inlay. She's seen better in student squats! And as for the bamboo picture, for goodness' sake...

The wall behind the picture has taken on the texture and contours of a massive plate of mould.

She tries to step backwards but her feet are sinking, deeper and deeper into the black stickiness that the carpet has become. She smells oranges but they are rotting. It is past the time for fleeing and no, she does not want to stay! She does not want to see!

She concentrates on her fear. Though she has no lungs, she gulps a breath and then another. Makes herself feel the terror in her body, an increased heartrate and tensing muscles. Makes herself tremble, makes herself feel the—

PAIN

She is so far back in her memories that a mere suggestion is not enough to wake her. It takes an external shock.

And Wander wakes.

***

She ricocheted into waking, the application of clamps to tender skin scorching down sleep-baffled nerves. The shock repeated itself at her wrists and ankles as she writhed, until Roscoe's voice got through, until she felt his hands against her face and in her hair. His wonderful, soothing voice told her she was safe, she was here now, that he had waited until she began to toss and turn, then did as she had asked. Was she okay?

Slowly she relaxed, though every muscle was now aching. She was naked and tied to the bed, once again drenched in sweat.

"Jesus," he murmured, stroking her now between the clamps. "What the hell happened?"

"I went home," she said.

"Wander, if the therapy... if you're still having these nightmares, I don't know that it's working."

Child.

"Oh, but it is," she said. "And I need you to do more, now. More than I've ever asked before."

***

Another week passed. The days, or so it seemed, grew incrementally colder, the nights incrementally darker. The same day a fringe group claimed the Socialists were planning to implement a secret tax for the establishment of mosques, there was an influx of children into hospital wards across the city, all during the same hour of the night. The children, ranging between seven to ten years of age, were all in the hypnagogic state associated with severe night terrors: screaming and thrashing, but not properly conscious. Some took hours to stabilise.

***

Friday, almost fifteen-hundred. Madeline sat in her chair with her notepad open before her. The page was largely blank. It was only to be expected that, after last week's outburst, her interaction with Wander would be awkward. At least her patient wasn't quizzing her—unlike Giselle, her mother (who had called at breakfast), or the Centre's receptionist—as to what could possibly explain simultaneous terrors in so many children. An explanation would be found, she was certain. But at present, she had no idea what it might be.

At last, Wander spoke. "I rang my sister. She's fine, if you're interested."

Madeline smiled. "I'm sure she was glad to hear from you. What does she do?"

"A lawyer, these days."

Madeline nodded, and then she waited.

"I mean, it was just a phone call."

The window and the door were both shut, turning her room into a green cell. Madeline found she approved of this, to pin down her writhing patient... was that how the bondage worked? Abruptly, she sat back and uncrossed her legs.

Wander did not appear to notice. "Look, I'm sorry I shouted last time. It's just that I... I got really angry."

"I understand," said Madeline, and because in psychology as bondage there was no room for mercy, she waited and waited until Wander was practically one huge knot.

"It's shadowing me now," she burst out. "Night *and* day. I can feel it on me, like the stink's got into my clothes. I can't share a bed with Roscoe anymore: it's too dangerous for him. I never should have let him come with me!"

Madeline stood up and slammed her palms down on her desk. "Enough is enough. Wander, you asked me to help you."

When Wander turned to face Madeline, her green eyes were wet. She was clearly exhausted—and were those bruises on her wrists? Her jacket sleeves made it difficult to tell.

"First, understand that you didn't have to wait till now to see me: you could have called and asked for an emergency session. I keep slots free for that, every day." Then she hesitated. She wanted to suggest Wander go into care for a few nights, just to see her through the crisis. But all her instincts said that removing this patient from familiar surroundings would only delay what had to come.

Wander hissed and her shoulders jerked suddenly. "You're a good shrink, you really must be. If I'd known how good, I would never have started this. You've got inside my head."

"I can only assure you, I haven't. Look, if something in your past were to turn out to be different to how you remember it, nothing in the present would change. How could it? You would not be changing the past, just rediscovering it."

"But if it means I'm... oh, I know I'm not normal."

"If it means you're strong. That you have already survived."

"What if *I* did something wrong?" Wander needed to say it, so Madeline let her. "What if this was all my fault?"

"I know you're afraid of losing control. But blaming yourself for things you couldn't possibly help is just another—"

"My sister." Wander's voice came huskily. "What if I hurt my sister?"

Madeline did not flinch, but her heart pounded and in her head she heard the words (not the same words, not quite) her brother had said, and saw his back retreating down the hall, duffle bag bumping off his hip...

"...something worse? Even worse than all this?"

"Wander." Madeline forced her voice to calm. "Will Roscoe stay with you this weekend? Because that's what I want you to do: to stay home with him. Don't leave your studio unless it is to come here."

"Will you be here?"

"I will make myself available to you, any time that you need me." She gave Wander her direct mobile number.

When Wander left, once again at the appointed time, once again conducting her bizarre ritual, Madeline called the receptionist and asked her to tell Monsieur Bernard she was running behind and would need another half hour. She told herself it was down to Wander's parlous state, that she needed to interrogate her decision to send her home. But she knew she was lying.

It was when Antoine's arguments with their father escalated to shouting and slamming fists into walls that she had become his confidante. Though she was only ten, night upon night he had sat with his little sister, the only member of the family who would let him speak. Only so much later did she discover what his words meant, that the Black Dragons were active even in the late eighties. Some nights he had shown bruises on his face—one time she still could not recall without cringing: his swollen lip had split and started bleeding as he spoke. And because he asked her to, she had said nothing to Papa and nothing to Mama, until the morning he didn't come home.

Years in therapy, years of working through her guilt, accepting her own powerlessness in the face of his death and her parents' separation, and suddenly, it was like it happened yesterday. And she knew, then, that it was *Wander* who had gotten too close. Wander had accused her, the psychiatrist, of getting inside her head, as she, the patient, slid around in hers. Sometimes it happened.

What Madeline needed to do now was hand her over to some other therapist. Perhaps Dr Legrange would be willing—he did enjoy the creative ones.

She closed her eyes as the waves surged ever louder.

***

And Madeline dreams.

She glances at the patient record form, which is scrawled over thickly in black and red. "I'm glad you called me," she tells Wander, who sits across from her looking considerably more relaxed than at their previous session. Her hair is pulled back, completely clear of a face no longer hollow or lined with fatigue. Her skin is still white but so smooth it appears mask-like. Her eyes are the intense green of a young tree python, and share its slit pupils. Atypically, she wears a long, dark gown.

Madeline drops her gaze to the form again, squints to try and tease out the letters, which are neither English nor French. "So what have you come tell me? You know nothing you bring here will leave."

Wander smiles, in a manner quite disturbing. "I think I must have made you into a symbol—my sense of inner peace."

"Ha! You really are witty," laughs Madeline, "even in my dream."

"In your dream?"

Of course this is a dream, thinks Madeline. *I never received a call and certainly didn't catch the Metro in the middle of the night.*

"Obviously!" she replies. "I'm the one who's asleep... well, what do you know. I almost never lucid dream."

"Madeline." Wander is no longer smiling. "Is—is that *you?*"

"This is my room," she replies, glancing around at the minty walls. "And you are my patient. Who else would I possibly be?"

"Oh shit." Wander rises with an appalling grace.

"Calm down," Madeline says automatically, then laughs again. Even in her dreams!

"It *is* you! Of all people."

"Well, I'm sorry if it's such a disappointment."

"Madeline, can you make yourself wake?"

"I don't know, I've never tried. I wonder if this dream is your influence on me?"

"Of *course* it is and I'm sorry! So sorry! All I needed was your damn room!"

"What are you talking about?"

"You told me yourself. To dream about something I need a strong emotional connection. The kind you get from picking at your old wounds for six weeks running." Wander glides towards the window. "How are we going to wake you? You could have jumped out the window, except... well."

What has become of her window? In place of the shutters and orchids is an unbroken expanse of pale green wall. Within it, there seems to be knobs or protuberances carefully camouflaged in olive and verge.

"You came to me," she says, "Because you wanted to dream about my *office?*"

"It had already found mine! Look, I know you don't understand anything that I told you about controlling dreams, but that's what I've been doing all this time. Creating a place I never see the outside of: a single, closed location connected to nothing else in my life."

"Therapy is connected to all your life, I'll have you know!"

"Oh, but nothing *leaves* here, remember? And the only symbol it connects to is the leaf—you don't know about the leaf, I never told you. But every time I come here, it's the last thing I see before Roscoe puts the blindfold on me."

"I don't need to know any more about your games!"

"It's no game."

Madeline looks again at the wall. The forms are resolving into hooks and straps, chains. Some kind of net is suspended from the ceiling. There is no door.

"Phobetor is coming, Madeline. I led it to the leaf and now I'm just waiting for our session to end. I should snap right back to our studio because that's what I see when he takes the blindfold off! But if I don't, Roscoe will wake me. What should happen is that Phobetor will be stuck in a green box, with no way forward. For the first time, It should lose my trail *completely*."

"In my office."

The consulting room seems shadowed now, though *sans* window or door, this is hardly surprising. The new furnishings are coming ever-clearer; it indeed resembles a trap, a room-sized snare. But before her, the patient's chair is now occupied by a crudely-shaped mound, like a human figure both rotted and burned.

"You sick bitch!" She recoils.

Wander writhes. "That's not one of mine."

Madeline gazes once more around the dungeon her room has become, and she knows it's ridiculous. The bare idea that she and Wander could share a dream! The tone of the walls is now way too dark, and the paint surface is rising in blisters.

"Try to shout," orders Wander. "To scream. Smash your hand against the desk—here, I'll do it!" Instinctively, Madeline ducks. As Wander lunges—no, as she *flows* towards her—the ceiling begins to sag. It looks like a plate of white mould. Droplets form on congealed and fibrous tips, shuddering foul and heavy before they fall, bursting on the dissolving rug. The back wall is blackening, as if in a fire. She can *smell* the foulness, the rot. She stares past Wander, at the body. The contours suggest the remains of a nose, and by the sockets of eyes, she knows it's Antoine. Not as she remembers him, but the way he is now. She wants to scream. She tries to scream but no sound comes.

As the wall breaks down into long, flaking tatters, borne upwards on the fretting air—or do they curl like fingers, do they flex, extending into her room like a gigantic hand? Some of Wander's additions begin to tilt and slip. The blackened wall folds outwards, becoming a cowl. Beneath it myriad forms tremble in and out of existence.

Her desk is disintegrating. *I want to wake up,* she recites silently as the filaments grope towards her. *I want to wake up.*

Then Wander stands between them. But she looks even less human than before. She rears and roars a challenge part avian, part ophidian, part nothing Madeline has ever heard. Shreds of the black gown lift and writhe. Wander's hair thickens into a hood like a cobra has. She is smaller than the dark eidolon above—but there is no mistaking the resemblance between parent and child

Phobetor's serpentine tatters, its beast claws and bird wings play fondly about the sphere claimed by Its child. But It has spent far too long searching her out in the shallows and now she must come home. She must understand where she belongs.

Too much, thinks Madeline, or rather, she fails to think. She can no longer stand. The sand is slipping from beneath her feet, crash and spread, crash and spread....

She feels the waves before she sees them. As they burst into the room, through the weakened walls (how had Wander ever imagined they would trap this thing?), there is no way to avoid them, nowhere to run; she can only fall as they take hold of her ankles. She is ready to drown as her brother did. She feels herself being swept away.

Bony wings burst out of Wander's back as she wraps the doctor in her own tatters. As the waves hit, Wander flaps, attempting to rise, but she cannot drag Madeline clear. She is forced to go with the current as it sweeps them out of the building and into a square ringed with trees, the fountain at its centre drowning as they are pulled past the border into the great universals of rage, grief and the unknown. Wings beating strong and with defiant carolling, the dark child keeps Madeline alive.

⁕

And Madeline and Wander dream.

The beach is long and blinding white. It is made entirely out of human skulls. The clear, aquamarine water laps at ear canals and teeth.

"Is this that beach you told me about? Oh, we are so fucked."

Madeline looks at Wander, seeing the green-eyed woman in the dark gown once more. The tatters have settled, the hood resolved into hair, but nonetheless, she attempts to scrabble backwards. But she finds she cannot move, cannot cause so much as a single skull to rattle. She tries to say, *What are you?* And perhaps her lips move, because Wander answers.

"My name is Wander Paxton. I was born in Sydney, Australia, but I've lived in Brisbane, San Francisco, Singapore, Guangzhou, Los Angeles, Budapest and Paris. I like Paris. I would very much like to get back there before Roscoe gets frightened enough to take me to hospital."

"What?" It is a small sound, little more than a squeak. But Madeline hears it, hears herself speak in a very deep dream indeed.

Where is 'here'? The beach at Toulon, only as she has never seen it. As she's always seen it. If she turns around, will there be shops clustering about the fountain?

"The waves were so strong, so vivid that they went beyond symbol. You tapped into an archetype and carried us into the deep. Where Wander trod, the skulls chinked and slid. So much power. Are you sure you're entirely human?"

Madeline is quite sure, so she nods.

"That may be so. But look where we've ended up."

When Madeline turns her head, she does not see the shops. She sees a vast chasm in which stairs lead to other stairs, through archways to other paths, down colonnades to courtyards glinting with fountains and twined with crimson flowers, where bridges compete with aqueducts and architraves to span their own, lesser voids, where the figures may be statuettes or colossi and a single bloom assume the scale of leviathan's mouth. Is that an orrery, cycling brass rings atop a pillar?

...an entire solar system, with scattered rings of asteroids and clouds of gas...

And beyond all that, is the palace. Oh, the palace rising amidst the waves of cloud with its curling spires and perfect, scrolling walls, mother of pearl and the scent of dying cereus...

"Beautiful," croaks Madeline.

"You think so? I see it differently."

Madeline gazes at the pinnacles laved in golden light. Were Wander not interposing herself, she thinks she might be able to rise and run, so long as it was in that direction. It can't really be that far...

But she is a trained psychiatrist. Instead of succumbing to the palace's unearthly allure, she pulls what she can of herself together and puts a question to Wander. Wander is silent, then, for what seems a long time.

"I'm Phobetor's child," she answers at last. "Whatever that means. I was created in that place, tormented and trapped there. But I escaped. It was hard. I think I broke myself doing it." A shadow passes over her pallid face, or is it merely the surge of what lies behind it? "But that made it easier to come all the way."

"All the way?"

"Awake. I know I'm not explaining very well. I've only just started remembering, and what I do, isn't good."

"Well, then," says Madeline. "I guess I did my job."

"You did, at that. And now we're here in the deep dream." Wander sits down beside her, dislodging several more skulls. "You live with someone, right? Someone who'll notice if you don't wake up?"

Madeline swallows. "Giselle. She'll come home." And then she thinks, *Giselle could come home late and find me already asleep. She could leave for work without waking me.* Panic flutters somewhere inside her nebulous sense of herself. "Can't you push me out of a window or smash my hand?"

Wander's voice is gentle. "That won't work out here."

"What about the leaf?"

"No, that's been sacrificed. What about you? Can you conjure more waves?"

Madeline considers. Shakes her head. "The waves… I can still feel them. But they've receded."

"We'll have to walk, then. And we need to be cautious. There's no telling where Phobetor might be, whether It was swept along with us or is still back in the dream of Paris, waiting for us to try and wake. We'll go through *your* dreams. It knows mine too well."

Madeline gulps. "I don't know how to do this. I can't even stand up."

Wander smiles. Madeline thinks there are fangs in it. "Here, let me show you."

✳✳✳

And Madeline dreams.

In an uncharacteristic hurry, Madeline patters down the stairs into the Saint-Sulpice Metro station. She is very late: Giselle will be home and there is no time to even grab a bottle of wine and some flowers.

She's running now. Below her feet the rumbling grows. The wind rushing from the tunnel brushes her face but she is still on the steps, which are cascading down, down; she is going to miss the train.

And then she is on the train, but the doors and windows are sealed and it is speeding impossibly fast in the wrong direction. She has not escaped. At the last moment, Phobetor has found her—and now she is being carried faster and faster towards a light, a white-hot blaze that progressively swallows each carriage, even as she tries to run, forgetting all that Wander has taught her, running faster and faster to less and less result—

And Madeline wakes.

Thrashing, gasping; leather tongue in a desert mouth. Heaviness across her legs: she kicked and something stung her arm as electric angels screeched into the void, *fiat lux!* She blinked and blinked as the white light poured in. A familiar voice cried, "Madeline! Where's the doctor? Hurry, get him!"

Warm arms wrapped around her. She tried to speak but all that came out was a sawing rattle. That wasn't right; she'd been talking to Wander just fine, once she stopped being self-conscious.

Wander, she thought, and stopped struggling. *I left her—is she all right? Did she make it back?*

"It's all right, dearest." Giselle stroked her hair. "You're awake."

And Madeline remembers.

Wander, black hair rippling like a nest of snakes, leads her down a black, volcanic slope where stand the petrified forms of men and horses, women, children and small bears. Their texture is glassy, the detail extends the smallest line upon the palm, but all readings reveal the same fate.

"Can you focus on my hand, Madame?" The doctor's face was pink and sagging. "How many fingers am I holding up?"

A hieroglyphic glade, where deer with flaming antlers pick a path through trunks that spell different words from different angles. Green snakes offer punctuation, but Wander warns her, they can be misleading, changing the meaning of the sentence-glades as they slide and twist.

Ice in her mouth, just shards of ice. "They want you to take it slowly, dearest. You've been on the drip for two days."

Two days? In a—in hospital, of course.

The delicate scrape of black claws across her skin. A cold, black beak emerging from a woman's lips and dipping into her mouth; oh yes, it is horrifying, it is perverse but so, so sweet...

Madeline shivered. And then, her mother's face was bending over her, drawn and faded but still that primal anchor. The sensations of the dream were smothered by the press of soft lips on her forehead, a gold cross spinning and winking before her eyes.

"There's my girl. My fine, brave girl."

"I'm all right," she said, and this time the words came out.

She had woken, fortunately, before it was deemed necessary to insert a feeding tube into her stomach. The IV drip was intrusive enough. When the pink-faced doctor came back to draw fresh blood samples, she asked for it to be removed. He bargained with her: what she could recall in exchange.

She told him she remembered taking the Metro home from work as usual. That she had been tired, it had been a long day with troublesome clients, but she had noticed nothing out of the ordinary. Giselle had been out, so she had made herself an omelette. Then she went to bed.

"Nothing else? No threats, say, from your patients?"

"No," she said.

"No one accosted you on your way home?"

She shook her head, feeling the itch of her dried-out hair, and wondered what he was suggesting.

Giselle held her hand as her mother fussed over her. "Your papa is in Abidjan," she said. "I've had trouble contacting him but I'm sure he'll be here as soon as he can."

"I feel fine," she said. "Hungry."

They let her eat consommé and a little jelly, and then the nurse advised that the ward was closing.

The lights dimmed as the visitors around other beds departed. The occupants retreated under their coverlets, and now fear slid through her. "I'm not tired," she said. "Really, I'm not. Can't you stay?"

"Your mother may stay," said the nurse, "for a little while."

***

And Wander dreams.

She coils around Madeline to hold her still, as the lava leopard passes, seething and dripping obsidian. A wonderful sight, but she feels Madeline holding her breath in fear. The creature slides away down a crevasse, but shortly after Madeline realises that she still isn't breathing, and things are difficult for quite some time.

Wander unfurls just a little of her wings, sends out just a few of her serpent tendrils, because the clouds above are challenging their passage. Big, bruised thunderheads with gnashing teeth; before her display, they melt away like ice in fire. She crows, and sees that Madeline is shuddering. Wander feels both contrite and annoyed—surely her companion has gotten used to the tatters by now!

Madeline, asking in all seriousness what her dream form looks like. Then accepting a kiss.

They re-enter Paris through Madeline's border, stepping into the square of Saint-Sulpice. She is vaguely aware it is near the medical centre, though obviously she has never seen it. In Madeline's dream, it is very beautiful.

Leaving Madeline to find her own way awake, Wander pushes onward through the familiar façade of sunlit Parisian streets. This close to the river, they are lined with linden trees just beginning to turn and a thousand figments surround her, slipping past her in sunglasses and broad hats. A street artist performs a classic mime routine up the side of a building: further along, another sits framed as a living Mona Lisa. As the topmost leaves split into valved wings and flutter away, all is vivid, fresh and bright.

Where might Phobetor hide? Does It seethe in the tunnels beneath her feet? Writhe behind those latticed windows, those creamy blocks of stone? Has It flattened Itself to a dark mist, beneath the trees of the Parc de Saint-Cloud? Or is it truly possible that the waves washed it back into the palace?

She cannot take the chance: she dares not fly or summon a door, do anything to cause the slightest change in her surrounds. Even a footprint could give her away. So she contrives to glide. A constant about-to-fly that keeps her feet from landing, while not revealing herself otherwise—from Saint-Sulpice, she makes her way slowly over the Pont du Sully. The Pont des Arts is closer, but its dream form is barred by the reflection of a thousand locks.

Nothing challenges her. Beneath the bright surface, nothing stirs.

And now she is finally racing faster and faster, down the alley and through the door and into the room where Roscoe sits—she sees him in the dream, sees him look up at her approach, then stand, face a medley of terror and hope as *he* sees her.

"Is it you, Wander? Are you back?"

"You're dreaming. Did you fall asleep watching me?"

He glances back down at the bed: to his body, she supposes, alongside hers. Meets her gaze again in wonderment.

"Is this what you do, then?"

"Yes, my love. But now we must both wake. And you must blindfold me again and take me down there."

"But there's nothing there yet, just a few supplies I left when I visited. What if the rats have got them, what if you need a doctor?"

"I need to hide, my love. And I will tell you everything, share it all with you. But now, we must—"

And Wander wakes.

***

Madeline had been comatose for nearly two days. It took as long again to persuade the doctors to let her go home.

Dr Hamm, in particular, was not willing to accept the results of his own tests. *There must be something*, his grumbling implied. A hairline lesion in her brain. A malfeasance of her glands. But finally, she was on her way, laden with referrals and dire hints about post-viral syndrome. Mama was harder to shake, but at long last, she and Giselle were alone together in the old apartment where she could finally, properly moisturise her hair.

That was when Giselle told her why the doctor had asked her if anyone had threatened her and why the police would ask her the same.

Madeline sat on the kitchen stool, towel wrapped around her head, staring into nothing. Into a memory of impossible things. "My office?"

Giselle nodded. "There's no need for you to see it. Once the investigation's finished, the police will clean everything up—"

"Giselle, I *have* to see it. We need to go right now!"

So they did. They caught a taxi, then walked along the cool, white corridor to the door.

The sight that met Madeline's eyes robbed her of all words. A thick, black substance marked every wall, smeared across the mint-green, breaking here and there into the most horrible, hateful words and signs. *Balasko... niger...* all the words she was afraid of. Nothing had been spared—her desk tipped, the chairs shattered, her *pagnes* and papers flung about. All her orchids were dead, blackened as if by frost. The rug was beyond hope, with stains penetrating right through into the floorboards: she didn't know how they could ever be cleaned. How the stench could ever be lifted.

"What... what is this?" she managed to say. The stench of mould, of rotten cloth. The pervasive reek of burned flesh. "Did they use paint?"

Giselle whispered, "The police said it was burned into the wall, somehow."

"I don't know who could have done this," said Madeline, except she did. Silently, she gibbered, *Is Phobetor still here?*

Minutes went by, surely, of inhaling the fetor, listening to her own breathing and that of Giselle. Giselle looked exhausted, desperate, and why wouldn't she? What was it that Wander had said?

I can't share a bed...

All the places Wander had stayed in all those cities, moving constantly year after year. To keep ahead of It. "I can't come back," she said. "I'll never be able to work in here again."

***

Madeline took a deep breath and entered the number. Then she stood in the secure darkness of the dining nook, listening to a phone ring on the other side of the world.

Wander Paxton, E – R. And her sister, Realise. Those were the first notes she had taken when Wander presented, and Realise Paxton was a distinctive name. It hadn't been hard to track her down to a large law firm in Sydney. Even though in her picture, she resembled Wander not at all.

"Rel Paxton speaking, hello?" The voice, too, was unlike Wander's, pinned to a city and a stratum of that city.

For a moment, Madeline hesitated. Then nerved herself, once again. "Hello, Ms Paxton," she said, "We've not spoken before, but my name is Dr Madeline Diomande and I am calling from Paris. Your sister consulted with me recently."

There was too much space, too many connections between them for the pause to truly be silent. But she knew that Realise (her peachy plumpness and blue eyes aggressively glassed, cropped and jacketed), was sitting in her office, performing her own nerving. "Oh really?" The voice did not offer respect.

"I don't do this lightly, but Wander has disappeared. As you were down as her next of kin, I was wondering—"

"She's not here, and if you'd paid attention during her consult, you'd know that already."

"I am simply trying to confirm that she's safe."

"Look, Dr Diomande, I'd like to think you mean well. But I'm telling you, I can't answer your questions and even if I could, I wouldn't. These are private matters, and you are not my doctor."

"I've been to her address in Belleville: there's no one there."

"You think you're the first person to call me after one of her fly-by-nights? You're not, so here it goes. Please do not call this number again. Do not call my parents, if you have their number. If you do, a formal complaint will be forthcoming to—let's see, the French Psychiatric Society?—regarding your harassment and unprofessional conduct. Do I make myself clear?"

"You do. I apologise for troubling you—"

The connection broke. Madeline set her phone down on the table.

She had indeed been to the address on Wander's form: a warehouse conversion in an alley decked with bright graffiti. The front door had been locked: she had walked up to the thin band of glass that was the only window and peered inside. No blinds or curtains, no lights. All that met her eyes was an expanse of bare, wooden floor. No scorch marks, no slurs, no rot.

Wander had escaped. Had left her here with horror and ruin. Damn Wander, damn her artist-lover, and her rude, *rude* sister!

"Who was that?" Giselle emerged from the hallway, tousle-headed in her pyjamas.

"I'm sorry, darling. I didn't mean to wake you."

"Wasn't really asleep." She yawned.

"Tisane?"

As she went through the motions of kettle and cup, Giselle slung herself onto the lounge. "You didn't answer my question."

"A professional call, to Australia."

Giselle raised her eyebrows. "That's above and beyond, even for you." And yawned again.

"It's not something I'll do again." Madeline dangled the teabag. "In fact, I was just thinking. If I'm leaving the medical centre anyway, I should make it a clean break."

Giselle's face lit up. "That's what I've been thinking too! Have to get through the election, of course, but then I could put in for a transfer."

"To another desk? The wheels of democracy would grind to a halt without you."

Giselle smiled. "Maybe I could spin them in Marseilles, even London. Probably not Australia."

Something in Madeline leapt at this idea. Yes, get out of Paris and then keep moving, across the channel and from there, anywhere...

You always think that even the strangest, stupidest things make sense and there's always something you can do. That's what Giselle had said to her. Was running off to London *doing*? Wander had been running for thirty years, but she was Phobetor's child. What did Madeline Diomande mean to a god? Nothing beyond that momentary connection. Now Wander had severed that connection, and Phobetor, for all the damage It had done, had surely gone in pursuit. This was her home; yes, this clunky, old apartment! The home that she and Giselle had made. She looked around the kitchenette with its peeling paint and thought very clearly, *I do not run from nightmares.*

Finally she smiled back at Giselle. "We probably shouldn't be too hasty, to make a decision like that."

"Mm," said Giselle. In that moment, she looked like she would happily pack their bags and be off to Charles de Gaulle in the pitch dark. But then she said, "You're thinking of going back to university, aren't you?"

Madeline paused, feeling the weight of the words on her tongue. "I'm going to help the children."

And it was true. She hadn't been able to explain, when Giselle asked her, what could make so many children have nightmares at the same time. But she could now. Rather, she knew what had happened: they had all come too close to Phobetor as It scoured Paris for the runaway. *This* was what she could do: reach out to them and help them, finding words their parents and doctors could accept. Children exposed to the same horror as her. There was no one else who understood what they had gone through. No one else who knew.

Then she realised that she hadn't spoken in some minutes while Giselle sat there, hands gathered into her lap. Madeline looked at her, and for just one moment recalled the taste of Wander's lips. Something from a dream.

"This thing that happened to me," she said, "I can't promise it won't happen again. But I'm going to fight it, in every way I can. I'm going to fight for us."

Something stirred in those brown eyes. Like Giselle finally suspected Madeline of knowing more than what she'd told the doctors and police. But it passed, and Giselle just sat rubbing her wrist around and around, until finally she suggested they should at least find a new apartment.

***

And Wander dreams.

She dreams her new home; a circle of shadow and space.

It is dark here, both by day and by night. She has no concept of which is which, only that she sleeps and wakes. Wakes and then sleeps. Her dream-self is confused, unable to get its bearings within an anomaly that has nothing to do with her life, nothing to do with life at all. There is stone here, arches rising to an ancient vault. There is bone here. Empty eye sockets stare from niches in the walls. It is cold and the rags that wreathe her limbs, passing slowly about her like drifts of smoke, are barely enough to quell the urge to shiver.

But she is not alone.

"We're dreaming together again, aren't we?" Roscoe stands beside her, bare-chested as always. He lived too long in Los Angeles for his dream-form to have any concept of cold.

"Yes," she answers, "we are."

"Damned if I'll ever get used to this." He looks around the chamber, like he sees Avalon or El Dorado, then says, "And you're sure it's safe? Your father won't find us here? Mother? How does that work?"

Did she grow, perhaps, from a drop of sweat or a trickle of blood upon fertile ground? What else was possible? The sheer will of something to reproduce, to fashion something smaller and finer than Itself to imprint and torment.

She answers the question she can. "We are far from the studio, across the river. And no one dreams of this place save us."

"You said you feel it when Phobetor is coming, so yeah, okay. If you say It doesn't know about this place, then, yeah, that too." He turns his face towards the vault that holds up unguessable tonnes of earth. "But *is* it safe?"

She focuses on that; a fear she can address. "Structurally it's sound, and as far as ventilation and seepage, I've seen worse in rental properties."

"Can you see the way out?"

"No, not yet." Wander gazes at the stone walls. Roscoe has done so well. He has saved her, in so many ways. "I can't ask you to stay here."

He sighs, so beautiful in his gleaming bronze. "And yet, here I am." He looks around. "Reckon it has potential."

The promise of warmth infuses her. "You have plans for this place?" She comes to him, coiling just a little. "Tell me what they are. Or better, show me. Make it change."

"It doesn't work for me," he mutters. "You know that."

"It will. Come on, try." She slips around his neck, and he shivers.

"Here's the thing. I know we have to keep our heads down now. But once the danger's passed... I reckon we could make something of this. Let some other people join, kindred spirits—"

"Then they would know the way and Phobetor could find –"

"Yes, yes: I understand. But I've been thinking about symbols, and what you can do with them. And it seems I've really been limiting myself."

"How so?"

"Why use a canvas when you have an entire catacomb?"

***

And Madeline dreams.
Madeline stands in the square of Saint-Sulpice.

It is a beautiful place in a city of beauties, a moment of calm and stillness within the constant rush. The white façade of the church itself, twin turrets rising into the sky like a guard or gate, the Fountain of the Four Bishops dignifying the paving before it—the tinted paving, with its hints of pink and green. How often has she seen this place in the midday light, or as now, wrapped in evening's chasuble? She used to have lunch here, and often made a special detour on her way to the Metro, just to take it in. Yellow light pours from the windows of the town hall and the café across the way. Now she stands so close to the fountain—closer than reality would ever permit. She could reach out and touch it. But even dreaming, she would never dare such familiarity with these marble gentlemen, seated so pensively in their niches. One can never truly be casual in the presence of the bishops, or of the guardian lions that sit with water spilling down their backs and splashing into the green angles of the pool. The bare branches of the chestnut trees are misted pink, and the sky is a pale mauve ribboned with pearly cloud. If she turns around, she will see the street leading past the town hall, to the medical centre.

No. No, that is not good. She should not be here. How did she come here—by Metro? Or did she find a symbol...? Because of course, this is a dream.

And in this dream, someone *is* watching her.

It is easy to be brave standing in the kitchenette with your lover, the sound of the news on television underscoring your tête-à-tête. It is easy to break down phenomena into current science, concoct proposals, and send to an old mentor. In a dream, it is harder. She glances around the square, in every direction but that. Creamy old hôtels with slate roofs, the classicism of the civic building: she is alone, save for the scattering of pigeons. Didn't Wander tell her that this was where her border lay? She starts walking towards the church, hoping to create distance between herself and the mint-green room she must never, ever enter again.

There, out of the corner of her eye: a figure stands at the junction of Rue Bonaparte and Rue du Vieux Colombier. She can make out no details, just the concentration of shadows. Perhaps it wears a beret, or its hair is cropped. She halts, panic seizing her—limbs? Her stomach? Her sense of herself is twisted in knots. Wander had assured her that in dreams she looks exactly as she does when awake, but that dark shape is not Wander.

It reminds her of Antoine.

She turns back to the church, convinced it is her only sanctuary, but she has forgotten her lessons again. Her effort takes her everywhere but forward. She finds herself veering towards the café and the medley of memories it holds, towards the flowing steps of the town hall. She gropes for the discipline Wander taught her, but her terror brings it all back—the stench, the melting of every clean form—which only drives her faster and harder away from the layered arches; the two, exquisite towers with their bells. She backs into the fountain, determined now to break all protocol and cling desperately to those stony knees.

Until she realises that the statue before her is not the genteel Massillon, but Charlize Theron in a bishop's robe, and she is standing in the bar that young Madeline used to run off to with the express intent of driving her mother mad. And then her mother is standing there, telling her that liking girls is only a passing phase and in due course her body clock (ironically enough, it is the chunky brass one that Giselle brought to their bedroom) is bound to go off....

A dream. Just a perfectly ordinary dream.

***

A week passed. Then another. The election was resolved with a great deal of shouting and posturing, but little actual violence.

A month passed, then another. From autumn to a sere and bone-white winter, and thence to pink buds and a mist of green.

A year passed. And there were impassioned demonstrations, bomb threats and exhibitions, orchestral recitals and football games that came down to the last minute. People ate samosas, danced and drank. Fireworks painted the sky with sparks: same-sex marriage was legalised in May and two of Giselle's friends held a marvellous ceremony which she and Madeline attended. Throughout it all, Paris remained Paris.

Madeline forced the faculty to accept her proposal. She gave the children's parents no choice but to listen to her. All showed signs of severe to moderate trauma, all were receiving a gamut of treatments which she examined, collated, and promptly began adjusting. Some responded to improved sleep hygiene and prescription drugs. Others did not, and to these she devoted her days and her nights. A radical combination of art therapy and mild hypnosis led to pictures with strange similarities, but also to a basis for image rehearsal therapy which finally began to show results.

She would not give up. This was what she was here to do.

***

It was a chilly evening in the final weeks of winter. They were meeting Madeline's parents for dinner, in a restaurant her father favoured when he was visiting from Abidjan. It had been a while, too, since they had gone out together, what with her cases and Giselle's own increasing workload. But for her mama and papa to be in the same room, at the same table, was a rarity, and she wanted Giselle to share it. Truth be told, she also wanted Giselle to bolster her against her parents' natural and well-meaning concern.

"So I'm finally meeting your father," Giselle said, closing her jacket against a wind that had emptied the marketplace in the Goutte d'Or. "They'll probably think we're engaged."

The possibility had hovered between them, ever since they attended the wedding of Giselle's friend. Madeline knew Giselle wanted to get engaged, or at least sign a Civil Solidarity Pact. She still wanted to move out of Paris, or at least Montrouge. They had looked at a few rentals, but then Madeline had just got so busy—and besides, neither action would address the real problem, which was the fear Giselle had carried ever since those dreadful days and nights. Finding her lover comatose and discovering the destruction of her office would certainly have been traumatic—Madeline had held her, encouraged her to talk, done everything she could to help Giselle work through it. She had gone so far as to offer to recommend someone, if Giselle felt she needed professional help, but this offer had been curtly refused. If she had a problem, Giselle had said, then she would find her own way of coping.

Since then, Giselle had been staying out on Friday evenings and Saturday nights, coming home at three or four in the morning. Following a lead, Madeline was told, or otherwise that she was with friends from work. They had been skipping their dinner-dance, even when they both were home.

The restaurant was warm and homey and did a decent okra and eggplant stew. Mama and Papa had chicken in kedjenou (though Mama was critical of its composition) served with fatty rice.

Her parents may have been well-meaning. They may have been as attentive as Giselle's parents, as aspirational as Wander had described her own. But they had been broken down by fate—by the unwitting conspiracy between a restless teenager and a naïve child. She had never been able to look at them like this before, to consider the impact of Antoine's disappearance so dispassionately. The great waves of emotion were still in recession, barely a whisper in her ear as she accepted her father's queries about her health, likewise his assurance of continued prayer.

She listened to his work stories, and told him about her work with troubled children. They were duly impressed, but it seemed to trigger something in Papa who, after a glass of wine, brought the spectre to the table. He reminisced about Antoine's fondness for a good kedjenou, of his popularity with the girls and his great gift for study, which was nothing Madeline recalled herself. Mama pressed her lips tightly together as he spoke, but her subsequent news about family friends and Madeline's old schoolmates seemed to involve nothing but children, born and expected, or doing so wonderfully well. Madeline let it wash over her, observing it all from a safe remove.

That was when Mama turned to Giselle and asked if she wanted children.

Till now, Giselle had dutifully held up her end of the conversation, but after a few non-specifics she grew silent. They ordered hibiscus tea as Papa began speculating on what Antoine would have achieved by now, had he lived. He would have become an engineer or a successful architect. Of a certainty, he would be married, indisputably have children of his own. When was his little girl going to have children, to show him a grandson with all of Antoine's gifts?

At this point, Madeline remarked cheerfully that Antoine had always been very fond of swimming. The three of them ended up reminiscing about Toulon and how beautiful it always was there. How much they wished they could all go back.

As family dinners went, Madeline thought this one a success. But as they were walking back through the icy, black market, where streetlamps stripped the concrete to the bone, Giselle burst out. "So that's why we never got a PACS! You haven't even told them about us, have you?"

Madeline attempted to soothe her: there was only so far you could go with some people, especially hardliners like her father. But Giselle seemed determined to take this personally. Standing in the street, she accused Madeline of exactly the kind of distancing she had experienced at the table, preoccupied with her work at the expense of all else, and before she knew it, they were arguing about everything.

"And where do you go each Friday night? Please don't try and tell me it's for work!"

"It was, originally." Giselle seemed suddenly a great deal calmer. "I told you I'd find my own way of coping, and I have."

"And does in involve drugs?"

Giselle drew a sharp breath and Madeline knew she'd crossed the line. But, those shadows under her lover's eyes, the slight dilation of her pupils in the morning, as they prepared for work. And now this. What was she supposed to think?

Knowing it was futile, she tried to continue. "If there's anything you feel you need help with—"

"Don't you dare criticise me! What about you!"

"What do you mean?"

"For fuck's sake, Madeline, just say it! Tell me what happened to your office. Tell me what made you sleep for two days!"

How could she do that? Her insights were for her patients alone. All those small, frightened faces, those tiny hands gripping at her hope, clinging to her words. Giselle hadn't shared the dreams, so how could Madeline possibly explain?

"People never admit to what they truly fear," she began, then her speech puttered out. *I'm standing here*, she thought, *while at any moment my love could slide away into the blackness....*

In sudden panic, instead of speaking, she grasped Giselle's wrist. Maybe she squeezed harder than she meant to, and Giselle flinched. Madeline let go immediately, staring in disbelief both at her own behaviour, and at what she saw. There was a pattern of bruising on that slender appendage that was somehow familiar.

"If you're not going to trust me," Giselle whispered, "how can I stay?"

Before Madeline could find any words at all, Giselle had turned and gone clipping across the deserted market towards the Metro.

Finally, words came. "It's not safe!" Madeline called across the desolation.

Within the week, Giselle was gone from their home and her life.

***

Another year passed. And there were parades full of pomp and glamour, protests against same-sex marriage, discoveries and austerities, once-in-a-lifetime concerts, strikes and a bad season of flu. On summer days, people picnicked in the Parc de Saint-Cloud, spreading blankets over the green grass, and for every couple that split apart, another came together. Of those who were dissatisfied with such mundanities, some explored other avenues and discovered other pleasures. Rumours circulated underground. A man unloaded a pile of manure outside the Palais Bourbon, and Paris remained the dream destination of tourists from around the globe.

Madeline made the children well. There were those among them, the talented and sensitive, who had never been normal, and this she did not interfere with. But she made them strong, able to express their passion as well as their fear. Some of the parents were not best pleased, even when she helped them, too, to sleep calmly. In the process, she offended doctors across the disciplines.

They said that Madeline's treatment of the child would only create problems in the adult. They claimed her reliance on mythical models was nothing more than bad Jung. They suggested she was too involved.

Two years is not a long time.

***

PARIS, 2015

It was Friday afternoon, at fourteen hundred precisely.

Dr Madeline Diomande smiled at her new patient. He was a skinny twelve-year-old with cropped hair and large ears. His skin was lighter than her own by degrees, but still a warm and healthy tone. His name was Farid Kateeb and he twitched and fidgeted constantly in his seat, accompanied by a low and breathless murmur.

She couldn't really blame him. These were the last weeks of summer and the air conditioning laboured in this corner of the faculty. Her new room lacked the spacious elegance she had once been used to; it was cramped and grey-beige, and the window looked out on to an alley. She had one decorative item, and one alone, that hung on the wall behind her.

The report in her hand stated that Farid's parents were shopkeepers in Barbe, concerned and attentive, but continually distracted by the demands of their business. Their son's symptomology only went back three months: he was not one of the original victims of Phobetor. He had not suffered such nightmares before, and there was no triggering incident—no accident, bullying or recent death among family or friends—that anyone could discern. But after weeks of screaming nightmares and fractured schoolwork they had returned from their GP with a referral to one Dr Diomande (who might be controversial, but she got results) and for the interim, a hefty Ritalin prescription. It did not appear to be working.

As she browsed the form, the boy jiggled his leg, making *pffhut!* sounds with his cupped hands. He wore the blue and red jersey of his local football club, and his knee was scabbed. Refusing to sleep at night, he had begun dozing off in the afternoon in class, and had on occasion been found asleep in odd places like the janitor's cupboard and once, the platform of the local Metro station.

"Hello Farid," she said. "I'm Dr Diomande."

The boy did not deign to reply, gazing at the ceiling duct.

"Do you train with the youth club?"

The murmuring became, briefly, audible. "Fuck yo bitch. Yeah, huh. Uh-huh." *Pffhut!*

"Oh, so you rap." She laid the form down. "You follow Booba or do you prefer the Americans?"

The boy stared at her, shocked into utter silence.

"My brother was into hip hop, right at the start." She was stretching the truth a little, but it was worth it. "He performed sometimes, locally. He wanted to go professional. How about you?"

The form said he denied any knowledge of his nightmares. Such denial had been characteristic of her original patients: telling an adult what they had experienced took a substantial leap of faith, as well as the development of a suitable vocabulary. So now she was treating more normal cases, she didn't attempt to force it. Rather, she encouraged the children to talk about their likes and dislikes, what occupied them in their waking lives. It didn't take her long to determine that Farid fancied himself an artist more than a sportsman, though the local club had his hearty support, and he did have quite the gift for rhyme. Her knowledge of the current hip hop scene was soon exhausted, but Farid proved happy to educate her, then to be drawn out into a wider discussion of school and home, and his circle of friends.

"My bros got my back, when it comes down the track, uh-huh. Keep on going."

The white-faced wall clock was ticking away the hour, so she gave him a gentle prod. She suggested that he used his rhymes to keep himself awake.

"Gotta say, gotta pray, gotta keep away."

"Keep what away?"

The boy didn't answer. Madeline gave him some space, then mused, "My brother said he would rhyme sometimes to make himself brave. When he really had to face up to something."

"If you say the words," said Farid, "you don't go there."

"So those are the *right* words. To repel...?"

"The Glider," he said, then paused, aghast. When the floor didn't drop out from beneath him, he continued in all but a whisper. "It wears a cloak with a hood so you can't see the face and there are all these snakes coming out all over the place."

Madeline felt like a sliver of ice had pierced her diaphragm. Her heart beat so rapidly that Booba, the righteous King of French Hip Hop, could have extemporised to it. She grasped for composure: fortunately, the boy didn't seem to have noticed anything. He had returned to his jiggling and cupping.

"Guess the... Glider doesn't like music," she said.

Pffhut! Pffhut! "Snakes go round and round and round, underground, underground."

The next step was usually to define which part of the dreamscape bore the taint of Phobetor's passage. Circling underground suggested tunnels: she took a deep breath and asked if there was any time, asleep or awake, he remembered visiting the Metro.

Pffhut!

"It's all right, I won't tell anyone. It's hard to control where you go in dreams, isn't it?"

Pffhut!

"Only, I think you're doing it already, with your words. Did you like going underground, before you met It there?"

"I like trains," he said. "They take you places. Lots of really cool places."

He was crossing the border. "I understand," she said, "but now It's down there and that isn't cool."

"Gotta say, gotta pray, *gotta keep away.*"

"Farid, you've been handling this situation really well. Using your words like that is very clever and you should keep doing it. But there are other things you can do that will help and make things less difficult for everyone. Can I talk to you about that?"

Farid eyed her, with regard for the fact she was making a kind of sense no other adult ever had. He came to a decision. "If you'll get 'em to stop them giving me the pills," he said. "They make me all muddled."

"I think that's a very good idea."

She and the boy talked for the remainder of the hour, about how breathing properly when you woke up could help calm you, as well as keeping the words flowing. Creating a firm break between dreaming and waking was a vital step, and what worked was different for each child. As promised, when his parents came to collect him, she advised them that Ritalin wasn't a suitable treatment in this instance, and they were better off accommodating their son's rituals within their own routine.

Once the Kateebs had left, Madeline started shaking uncontrollably. She swivelled around, her back to her desk, and stared at the painting that hung on the wall. The painting by Roscoe Keene.

***

And Madeline remembers.
She never laid eyes on Wander's partner, though she heard a good deal about him. From the catalogue for the exhibition at the Niche Gallery in Montmartre, he stares at her with cryptic, black eyes. He is lean but muscular, bronze-skinned and sporting a black buzz cut. Around his neck, on a leather thong, hangs a chunk of amber with an insect caught inside.

A spring rain falls this evening, and she has just submitted her first paper (*Nightmares as a symptom of childhood stress disorder*) to the faculty journal. At least some of the butterflies afflicting her stomach are from this, how this attempt to legitimise her theories shall be received. The rain makes haloes of the lamps outside: as per its name, the Niche is narrow but runs a long way back, through other buildings and into the hill for all she knows. But it is warm and smells of wood and orchids.

The owner is a bustling, pink-cheeked woman with a silvery bob: Madeline has no idea what the protocols are for the viewing and buying of original art, so she avoids her for now. She edges through the crowd of well-dressed banker-types and skinny, black-clad androgynes, seeking out exhibits twenty-two through twenty-four.

She may know little about art, but when she sees the three canvases, her breath catches. Roscoe's work jumbles recognisable shapes and words into mad conglomerations of colour, that when viewed from a distance take on their own, distinct identities. Two gloss the Paris skyline with Mansard roofs and spires; the outlines of a hundred Paris buildings overlaid upon each other and threaded through with signs such as 'Exit', 'One Way' and 'Detour' forming cryptic messages. But the third, the third is different. The technique is the same; even she can see that. But from his signs and silhouettes, his smears and odd half-forms like birds, people, and fungi, he has created a tunnel. The outmost layer is all smoke and gloom, but once the threshold is passed, colour explodes. According to the catalogue, the title is *Could I But Be Your Shadow*.

She knows what she is seeing. The painting speaks to her of a journey past a black mountain and a purple plain, a city, and a garden. Such emotions come flooding back; it is all she can do not to run back out onto the street, screaming or weeping. In the deepest part of the painting (only it isn't deep, of course, it occupies the same flat surface as all the rest), is a figure she knows.

What would they make of it, these people who surround her? The smudged, black wings, the trailing strands of hair and gown? They are like her parents. They are like Giselle.

The owner advises that these are works she has held for over a year. She regrets she is unable to help Madeline in locating Roscoe, whom she believes has returned to the US and gone off the grid somewhere in the Mojave Desert.

If Giselle was still with her, she would never dare purchase the painting. Even so, she doesn't dare bring it home.

***

Madeline sat alone in her shuttered apartment, the pipes banging somewhere behind the walls. Outside, the summer night pressed in like thumbs upon her temples.

Almost three years she had spent searching, and now a new child had described Phobetor to her on a sticky afternoon. *Had* the

Sovereign of Nightmares been washed away and finally managed to return from the deep? Or had It concealed Itself in the shallows until the time was right, and what would that mean? What was right about now? And why, really, would It have lingered here when Wander had fled with Roscoe to the furthest corner of the earth?

Maybe that was why. Maybe It had given up on its own child and was seeking to take another in her place.

A mad thought. As ridiculous as anything her peers had accused her of. But her pulse was drumming, and her hands were shaking again. If that were the case, what could she do?

Find Wander.

The kettle began whistling. With shaking hands, Madeline opened the box and took two attempts to drop the teabag into the cup. Then, changing her mind, she fished the bottle out and poured a finger of brandy instead. Steadied by the warmth in her stomach, she tottered across to the bookshelf and extracted a single manila folder from its camouflage of English magazines, the *Times* and *The Atlantic*—there were so many things Giselle hadn't bothered to take, which Madeline hadn't bothered to throw away. And this folder, the only thing she had bothered to retrieve from her ruined office.

Wander Paxton, E – R. What could possibly be in here that she hadn't discovered already?

Farid could not be permitted to suffer any more than he had. None of the children she had helped—not hers in any sense her mother would accept, but all the same—could go through this again. *Paris* could not. She had to do something. Perhaps after three years, Realise would be willing to talk and grant her some clue, some insight. But instead of picking up her phone, she kept turning the pages, week after week of instructions on how to move in dreams, how to travel using symbols, how to control their content. Warnings about the border. This formed the basis of her treatments, and she practised what she preached. She'd been so careful. When was the last time she had dreamt anything other than an anxious rehearsal of her daily routine? Haunted by the image of Giselle—a smiling, fading figment. Easy enough to blame it on fatigue, on the preoccupations of her work. But she could no longer pretend, could she?

The hood merging out of the wall. The black tatters reaching towards her, a distillation of every nightmare she had ever suffered.

Maybe her eyes were moist, maybe her breath caught, as she sat there on the lounge with the cup. She was thinking of how astonished her father would be if she arrived on his doorstep in Abidjan, having renounced her Parisian life, as the pages of scratchy handwriting finally revealed something other than Wander's dreams.

"A wine bar on the Rue de Raspail... signs of subsidence suggest a cavity."

It had come up in a discussion of Wander's work for the insurance company, one of her recent inspections. The ground in that part of Paris, she had said (with all the arrogance of the outsider), was riddled with tunnels from a hundred different periods. This bar might actually sit above something, if anyone could be bothered looking.

The bar was not named, in her notes. But Farid saw the Glider in the Metro and there were tunnels that passed close... this was crazy; she was only thinking this way because of the brandy and because the smoky fringes of Roscoe's painting (which she stared at every day), incorporated a sign reading 'Metro Mon—'. And creeping round the very edge, almost under the frame, was another message. *'Halt. This is the empire of the dead.'* It was the legend inscribed over the entrance to the catacombs. The catacombs, dear God! Was this a *movie*?

But what if the empty studio and all suggestion of deserts were merely blinds?

What if the reason that Phobetor was haunting the tunnels of Paris was that Its child had never actually left?

***

And Wander dreams.

Above ground, it may be day or night, but she suspects that it is day. Mid-afternoon, as Roscoe watches, she dozes in their sanctuary before the night's exertions. She glides through the dream of the Paris Metro, using her hover trick (which is now second nature) and wrapping herself in a thick layer of shrouds and stains. Not even her strongest willing could keep her sealed in forever—not once their guests began arriving, bringing with them all the scents and flavours of the world outside. No matter how cunningly Roscoe distracts her, the cleverness of what he has constructed, she will roam. But surely, this is safe enough.

She passes down tunnels of shadow eroded by the passage of dream-trains. By night, a million sleeping commuters rehearse the race that awaits them come morning: it is even better camouflage than an airport or a crowded street. And of those dreams of passage, *all* overlap in just a little way. She knows this now: how many times in the past did she write off the presence of another dreamer, merely because their impact on the dreamscape did not match her own? She appreciates, now, the subtle things. The sofa manifesting in the dark haze of an otherwise empty arch—another afternoon dozer, slumping half-off the cushions? The scrawls cut into the grimy occlusion caking everything here, the residue of depression and boredom—someone nodding off at their desk in the middle of work? She glides past these tokens and over the glinting suggestion of rails. Nowhere does she actually sight someone—that remains a rare and special circumstance. It demands a connection such as she has with Roscoe, or formed during those six strange weeks with Madeline.

Madeline Diomande, like a little sister grown wise enough, strong enough, to defend herself. She had defended them both, foiled Phobetor with her own symbol. How how strong her grasp of dreaming had been! Wander appreciates now, just how rare Madeline's talent was. After three years of training, Roscoe still falters. Under no circumstances will she seek Madeline out. That would be madness. Besides, without a doubt the doctor left Paris shortly after their return from the deep: ran as far and as fast from Wander as she possibly could....

Wander stops reminiscing, before a door forms in the encrusted wall that might lead to the square of Saint-Sulpice. She can do that so easily now. But no, she must return to the sanctum, wake and prepare for the evening, even though the prospective sameness of this to every other waking chafes her. But discipline must be maintained. Three years is nothing, when hiding from a god.

In the very act of sweeping up her shroud, somethings stirs the dark aether. It falls upon her as a sound. Weeping? She has heard weeping in these tunnels before, many times. She has heard the muttering of vast crowds and percussion like to a bouncing ball, passing endlessly from wall to floor and back.

But this is chanting. The rhythm not of a ball, but some kind of mantra, and this too she has heard before. Once, in a moment of weakness, she followed the sound a way, pulling back only as she realised how much cleaner the walls grew, how close she must be to the bright dream of Paris. This time she does not move, and still the chant draws closer.

She pulls the shroud over her, becoming deathly. Exactly how she appears when doing this, she doesn't know, for Roscoe stays awake. But it has to be less like herself. Hovering here, waiting for the elusive voice to manifest is against the rules: Roscoe will have to punish her tonight. But she hovers still, because after all this time, she *wants* to see another dreamer. How clear or hazy they are compared to him and to Madeline, what kind of control they possess. Is that really so bad?

The chanting grows louder and she realises that, after all, it is different to the last time. The same words but the tone of the voice has changed to something at once higher and rounder. But it is too late now to flee, as a figure coalesces in the smoke. A figure that steps between each sleeper so slowly and deliberately they must fear tripping. Their edges are perfectly clear, as are their colours: deep skin and dark hair, wearing a black T-shirt and beret. Wander expands, becoming a layer against the wall, but it is not enough. The figure stops in the middle of the tunnel, staring at her with an expression of shock.

"Oh... my... God."

Wander finds a tongue, of sorts. "Halt," she rasps ossiferous. "This is the empire of the dead."

"It's you. Dear God, I thought Phobetor had returned... but it was *you!*"

"What the hell are you doing here?"

"Looking for you!" Madeline thrusts a finger in whatever her face currently is.

Wander feels her own anger rise. "Why did you come here? Are you drunk?" Out of the wall she writhes, shattering rib cage corsets and clavicular yokes. "Are you *high?*"

"You gave my patient night terrors," Madeline hisses, not giving an inch. "A twelve-year-old boy!"

"We can't do this."

"Why not?" Madeline challenges.

"You know why!"

"Phobetor's long gone! God, I've been such a fool—"

"Oh no. It's not."

"Then why isn't the whole of Paris screaming mad? Why am I still alive?"

"Regarding the first, I can't say." Wander settles onto the ground, on her own feet, and something sounds like a distant chime. "But as to the second, well. Have you considered It might be waiting for you to do exactly what you've done?"

All around, at the very periphery of her senses, it seems tracks are starting to shift, rubbing against each other like giant snakes.

"We can't do this," she repeats urgently. "Wake yourself, then go, get out of Paris! It won't follow you, not now It knows I'm down *here.*"

The air is thickening just slightly, a condensation of ash and soot. No time to resume her disguise, and best she doesn't if she is to lead It a chase. To give Madeline time to wake and escape. She turns back to the wall and focuses on a symbol she has prepared— nothing that lies in the sanctuary itself, of course. And it seems Madeline has worked out what she's doing, because she cries, "Don't go!"

For one long and luscious moment, she considers bringing Madeline in. Keeping her safe behind the walls, introducing her to Roscoe. Oh, such games they would play!

But she will give Madeline one more chance.

"Still can't wake yourself? You should have a safe word." She flicks a black tatter flirtatiously towards Madeline's face.

The doctor recoils. "Go to Hell!"

She lashes out with another, snagging Madeline's feet—ah! The tingle of contact, the undeniable presence! A single jerk and down the doctor goes, smack upon the rails. Without waiting another second, Wander turns to the dark and carols, long and loud. Then she launches through the door forming in the wall and flips ninety degrees, tipping herself down a well of bones.

***

And Madeline dreams.

Wander is gone. Madeline saw her open a door in the smeared wall. A strange door, this—like something from the deep dream, she watched her fall through into a circle of perfect black. But for an instant, the black was ringed by grinning, grey skulls interspersed with the carious ends of femurs. Then both the vision and Wander were gone.

Madeline sprawls on a pile of velvet dust, in a tunnel now as dark as night. Despite the shock of falling, she is still asleep.

She knows where she is, or at least in which dream. Metro and catacombs, the whole myth of the Paris underground. This is what she gets for falling asleep over her brandy, obsessed with a painting and Farid's nightmare. The tunnels around her are labyrinthine, and every surface is coated in soot.

She picks herself up and begins walking, in the direction of away. Her surroundings do not alter, no matter how hard she concentrates on taking actual steps, but at regular intervals, the wall breaks in an arched recess about a metre deep—in the real Metro, it would be a shelter for railway workers. It sears her to think of Farid, a skinny figure in a football jersey, wandering this place and even glimpsing that terrifying jumble of bones and cowl. But if Farid found his way out, then she can too.

A dim fog seems to be rolling through the tunnels. At first, she thinks the thickening is her own trepidation. Then the smoke heaves and billows, and she inhales the unforgettable scent, a medley of burned flesh and sewer graves. She remembers the walls darkening and paint blistering, ceiling sagging like a plate of white mould.

Smash your hand against the desk.

Given that Wander had failed, she must do it herself. She tries to trip but the sleepers adjust unerringly to her feet. She turns her hand so the nails will hit first and flicks it against the wall. The surface slips away: gritting her teeth, she concentrates as Wander once taught her, forces herself to feel the greasy slip beneath her fingers, a prickling like ground glass. In both directions, the tunnel recedes gravelled and drear, with no indication of a break. Nothing but the endless repetition of arches—a thousand arches she has passed, all poured of concrete, and why that shape? An arch like a church doorway, like those running around the façade of Saint-Sulpice, no less. Some conceit of nineteenth century engineering. Graffiti is forming along the tunnel behind her, great letters swept out of the grime. *Balasko, niger, tache...* She sights the next archway and lurches towards it, thinking of shelter.

Against her foot she feels the rail vibrating. Oh no, no—is that a humming in her ears and is the smoke growing yet thicker? The arch opens and she has no choice; she must press against the wall and pray that the train, which will be no train, runs past her, that it somehow misses her. And the recess is dark and hideous, as the arches in Saint-Sulpice are white. She has stood before the cloister, so sweet and shady during hot afternoons, streaming with light on purple evenings as the sound of the choir rises within. If only this arch... could become that arch.

She has never done this before, but what choice does she have? She faces away from the tunnel, ignoring the roar and the shaking clinkers, and *remembers.* She *desires.*

She feels It running up the tunnel like an earthquake. Her feet slip on the gravel—she teeters, listening for waves, but all are gone. Instead... instead, the archway shivers.

You want this.

They are not words which slap her around. They are meaning, roughly distilled from something so much vaster. The mere suggestion hits like a thunderclap, oozes through her like cold current and she has no choice....

Standing framed by the arch is Antoine.

She starts to shriek, but this is not the charred and rotten corpse. This is Antoine with smooth, umber skin and hair as thick and rich as her own, fire in his eyes as he tells her, "I have to go out tonight."

This knows.

As the meaning recedes once again, leaving her gasping and choking, Antoine is gone. Instead, a bed stands upon the rail line in the very centre of the tunnel. A rusted, iron-frame bed with stained and flattened pillows. The man lying there seems trapped rather than sleeping: a man in his late forties, perhaps, once-pale skin now rusted and wrinkled, once-blond hair as threadbare as the sheet. Trapped in slumber, lungs labouring under a weight of dread. Is he one of her patients? A hostage, revealed to make her stay?

Across a withered bicep crawls a black tattoo, the swastika that never fades.

BROTHER inside. Again again again—

She shrieks, "*I don't care!*" And somehow, she turns and pitches herself through the arch, leaving the sleeper to his fate—and then she is no longer suffocating inside the tunnel. She has broken her fall against the rim of the pool, where stone lions snarl and paw as the water splashes and purls.

All is calm. All is quiet. The mingled sweet of chestnuts and coffee, leaching the taint from her non-existent lungs. She sags now to the paving, knowing this respite is temporary, that fleeing Paris is her only hope. For three years, Phobetor has watched her. All her bravery in staying, her attempts to heal those It had scarred, have played into Its hands.

And now she has finally served her purpose, It—speaks?

Suddenly, the realisation hits. That man she saw, that sleeper, was no hostage. She has never seen him before in her life. And yet, if that *thing* can be believed... he dreams of Antoine.

Why would he dream of her brother, that man so rusted and frayed? Of a young Antoine, strong and able, marching into the night?

There is only one reason.

She pulls herself up, resisting the urge to dust off the black jeans she wears for some reason. The light streams from the café, the pigeons weave and circle, or are they doves? Why not doves? A figure stands at the junction of Rue Bonaparte and Rue du Vieux Colombier.

She can flee into the back streets, back towards her home. Then wake and head for the airport.

She does not.

As she marches across the pavement towards It, the figure takes on the shape, again, of Antoine.

"Neither of you belong here," she tells It.

The figure stands, impassive.

"I can give you something that will take you closer. If you find her, will you go? Take her back to the palace and don't let her out."

Antoine nods, solemnly.

"Then that's all I want."

The figment of her brother extends his hands and it seems natural to take them. She concentrates first on the feel of warmth and slightly roughened skin. On the throb of a pulse. She concentrates as hard as she can, squeezing as if by this she can make him real.

Into that pulse streams every memory she has of the façades of bars along the Rue de Ravail. The sense of catacombs, of cracks running down, down, down. The image of a black disc circled by bones.

Antoine smiles.

And then the soft, mauve air is gone. The splash of the fountain: above all else, his hands are gone, when she had only just now found them. She is back in the tunnel—no, in a deep alley, sunk in trash and autumn fog, watching her brother move cautiously into the space opening before them. The intermittent wash of headlamps from some nearby road, the flashing red of a sign illumines him. He glances about, shoulders braced and each foot placed carefully in heavy combat boots. She sees his eyes widen, realising he is trapped in a blind end.

No, she tries to speak but can't. *I don't want to see this. Stop, please....*

Antoine catches himself up, attempts to retreat, but it is too late. She cannot see the enemy he confronts, but from his posture it is way too late to run. His face is set; he knows what's coming. Nonetheless, he puts up his fists as she... as *she* advances upon him.

*****

And Madeline wakes.

Choking, spluttering, aching. She had fallen asleep, it seemed, on the lounge with the brandy bottle beside her.

"What the hell, Maddy?"

Giselle was sitting on a stool close by, and she did not look happy.

Madeline put her hands to her temples. Her head throbbed and Giselle's appearance made no sense at all. She had seen her brother beaten to death through the eyes of a man holding a steel pipe. In a trash-filled alley, she had *seen* it. Again and again.... With an impatient grunt, Giselle thrust a mug of water at her. Madeline's mouth was parched: it was almost as bad as waking in the hospital. She drank and then tested her voice. "Giselle, what are you—"

"We're leaving. As soon as you can stand without fainting, 'cause I'm not going to carry you."

Leaving? Of course, she must leave, must run before It found her again and smiled on her again, her brother's smile. *A deal is a deal.* Giselle tilted her head, blonde hair wisping against her cheek. She looked thinner and a good deal harder than she once had. Broken blood vessels framed her nose, and her eyes had a glaze to them.

Madeline's heart quaked. "Here's the thing, Maddy: you were supposed to leave Paris after Wander spoke to you."

"Wander?" Madeline felt dizzy. Giselle didn't know about Wander. But then, Giselle shouldn't be here. Again she wondered if she'd woken at all, but the pain in her head was all too real.

"Oh for fuck's sake Maddy: do you really think I lived with you, shared a bed with you but couldn't see you were obsessed with this patient of yours? And then you brought her file home, even though it *smelled*. I thought for sure your BDSM bitch was behind the vandalism. Did you think I wouldn't investigate?"

"You *can't* know," Madeline said helplessly. "It's not safe!"

"No," said Giselle, "It's not safe. You were supposed to leave Paris yesterday."

Yesterday? She had slept—oh God, not again!

"But when I come by to check, here you are asleep! Asleep!" Giselle shook her head in outrage. "Now I guess I've got no choice."

"Giselle." Madeline reached out a hand. "Why are you here?"

"Because Wander seems to care about you." Giselle took hold of Madeline's hand and yanked her to her feet: Madeline staggered, but as Giselle dragged her towards the door, she resisted.

"You've met Wander." Madeline dug her heels into the floorboards. "Where she is? How did you find her?"

"You're still obsessed." Giselle stopped pulling but didn't let her go, rummaging in the pocket of her jeans with her other hand. "At least now I understand why."

"But you *don't* understand! She's not even human!"

"Oh, I know that." Giselle grabbed her wrists and with a neat *clip!* cold steel snared her. Madeline stared down at the handcuffs in disbelief. "That's why I'm going to all this trouble to bring you to her."

***

When Giselle pulled a blindfold over her eyes, Madeline shrieked.

"Stop that," ordered Giselle, pulling the seatbelt around her.

They drove for what seemed like hours and she was sitting in the front seat with a blindfold on. Hadn't anyone noticed, or didn't they care that a woman was being kidnapped in broad daylight? She could have struggled against the cuffs and screamed, but her head still ached and besides, what else was she going to do?

She is taking me to Wander. They have blindfolded me so I can't retrace the way in dreams.

By the time they got out (in an underground garage, by the tilt and bumps), her head was marginally better.

"Giselle," she said, as the seat belt loosened and she was pulled from the car, "I'm sorry I didn't tell you. But I never thought you'd believe."

"Maybe not." Giselle's grip on her shoulder tightened as the timbre of their footsteps changed. They were entering a smaller space. "But I'd have known you cared."

They lost the light quickly. From seeping grey, it was now black as pitch. In the absence of other stimuli, the images of her nightmare, a murderer's nightmare, cycled before her until she noticed things that had escaped her at the time. The disposition of the alley, the vestigial posters on the walls, the fog itself. Was it possible she could find it? Was it possible Antoine's body was still there?

Then without preamble, her escort pushed her down till she was hunching, waddling forward under what she sensed was hard rock. A hard hand cupped the back of her head. "Careful," said Giselle.

Light finally seeped back into her eyes as space opened around her. Then the blindfold was tweaked from her head, revealing a greenish blur.

A blur that, as the seconds passed, came to look more and more like a forest.

She was crouching in a rough-hewn passage (it *felt* underground, deep, deep down) where the walls were painted with impressions of a forest glade receding into lush verdure. White-capped mushrooms grew in the corners, amid sinuous, art nouveau bronzes that might have once been door handles or the stems of lamps. All were tarnished and broken. Tiny LEDs winked upon the twilit ceiling. As she looked, it became clear that both the glade and the sky were built up from a base of green and purple graffiti, snatches of poetry and single words—"BOSKY", "LUMINOUS"—in great looping letters. She had seen something like this before.

"This way," said Giselle. Madeline was pulled onwards.

The passage turned sharply, and suddenly she was surrounded by doors. Whereas the first section had smelt earthy, fungal, this smelt musty, like wood. Doors and windows, big and small, ancient and some quite new-looking, set at crazy angles and tilting overhead. Doors opening inside doors, carved with more words: this was stupid, like the fantasy gardens she had been dragged through as a child with dioramas of Santa and Snow White.

Around the next corner was—red. Just red (DESSICANT, PILGRIM), a passage drenched in crimson and perfumed with dragon blood resin. It was then Madeline realised what was happening here. What the tableaux were meant to represent. "Shit," she said.

The next will be black, she told herself. *Black and jagged for the mountains.* And she was right. Roscoe (for his hand was everywhere in this) had attempted to dress the passage to match the deep dream. It was like his painting but decompressed.

After the mountains came the plains. To suggest the endless vistas of rippling grass, Wander's lover had resorted to cloth. Layered, yellowed satin and mauve linen spotted with flowers, phrases spelt in embroidered monograms I WANDERED LONELY AS A, cloudy draperies of gauze all spotted with mould. It was old, all of it, weathered and stained, *buried.*

The floor of the next bend was lined with skulls. Honest-to-goodness domes of decrepit bone that had grown inside people. Black sockets stared up at her: *was* this part of the catacombs, she was entering? Some institution's private crypt? Something Roman that had been walled away and forgotten? She had no idea.

"Nearly there." Giselle guided her along a route providing the barest clear patches to place her feet. Not kicking stray bones demanded she keep her gaze on the floor. She felt space open around her once more but saw nothing of it until she was finally in the clear.

This chamber was huge and like the passage, lit by LEDs that threw shimmering pinks and golds upon the far wall. It looked like dawn rising there behind the pillars, here where dawn would obviously never come. Was the place an abandoned Metro station? A lost bomb shelter? Perhaps it was a Roman temple, with those pillars supporting the roof. When she made the mistake of glancing up, the ceiling seemed to bulge with an impossible, crushing weight. Whole buildings stood above her; apartment blocks, churches, offices... a cloying scent tickled her nose, comprised of dust, damp and musk, a sweaty fug sweetened with more incense. And across the floor stood a bewildering variety of objects, that at first defied identification.

Were those sculptures? At one time, yes. Partial bodies of marble, missing limbs and heads, the kind of thing that might have been dumped by indiscriminate builders or by people cleaning up after shelling. Chains had been draped around them, leather straps used to hold them together. And here was more classic art nouveau, a railing or grill set upright. She could see handcuffs, like those even now pinching her wrists, dangling from the edges.

Realisation dawned. She looked back at the sculptures and saw the straps were positioned strategically at the neck, waist and arms. Somebody could be *tied* to the marble.

I've found my own way of coping. That was what Giselle had said, after she began spending nights out on the town. A sick feeling twisted through Madeline's stomach, remembering the questions Giselle had asked when she learned about her new patient's predilections. She'd given Giselle the clue and never thought to follow it herself. A floor harp, an honest-to-goodness gold harp stood there, a little tarnished and missing half its strings. A deep flourish of colours snared her gaze; crimson, viridian and blue, surely a stained-glass panel from a demolished church, standing upright like the grill. The glass's central figure was missing but the outline was there, a vacancy with sharp edges meticulously cleared of lead.

Madeline looked down once more. A short distance from where she stood, swirling lines of green, bronze, red, black, and purple swept across the floor. Escapees from the passageway, looping out across the stone in intricate designs, knotting together in patterns that once again incorporated words, then shooting up into the air! Long cords, netting and straps dangled from a tripod that stood maybe a head higher than a tall person. It rose at the centre of this torture garden, like a sundial emitting rainbows.

Behind the silhouetted pillars, the light swirled. She understood, this was meant to be the palace. The place where Wander was made, where she was tortured and trapped. The place she broke herself to escape.

Why had she and Roscoe done this? The work of three years: impressive, yes, possessed of flair and ingenuity. But still a token, scrappy and even tawdry in places. A theme park of dreaming.

"It's a symbol," she said aloud. "A symbol of the deep."

"That's right," said Roscoe. With that accent, it just had to be him. He sounded pleased that she understood. "Did it all with findings, just things recovered from the tunnels and landfill. Lot of stuff tipped down here over the years."

She turned and looked at him, only to see a burnished leather mask. The skin of his chest and arms was paler than it had been in the catalogue, his hair and beard long and straggling, but he was no less muscular and lean. His only clothing was the same amber pendant and a pair of leather trousers that looked like they were laced on. "What the Hell are you doing down here?"

"Hiding." It was Wander who answered, but she would not look at her, not yet.

"You can't have just stayed down here."

"We get by."

"I contacted your sister, after you vanished. She doesn't want to know."

And into sight stepped the real Wander, hair loose and drifting, and Madeline's heart skipped a beat before she realised that the gleaming, black feathers were just another mask. Wander was wrapped in what looked to be *findings*. Dead pale, as if for three years she hadn't seen the sun, and maybe she really hadn't. Amongst the hair, some threads gleamed silver and her eyes, her eyes were sunken. Like the visage she wore in the tunnels, a masked corpse.

"What will happen when you die?" Madeline asked. Roscoe bridled, but Wander remained calm.

"I don't know," she replied. "But until then, I want to keep my family safe. That's why we're hiding, and that's why you should have left Paris." She glided closer. "You shouldn't have spoken to my sister, Madeline."

"So what now?" Her heart was pounding.

"You stay here," said Wander, "It's the only safe place."

Sickness roiled in Madeline's throat. This was horrible. The idea that this was their lives, that they had passed birthdays down here. And worse, that others knew about Wander and about this place and came here voluntarily… oh, of course, of course! That was why Roscoe had painted the walls and stacked the skulls. Wherever they came from.

"It's clever," she said, repressing a shiver as the masked man moved towards her. "The dreams people have of this place will look like the deep. Phobetor could pass right through them and never realise."

"That's the idea." Roscoe examined the handcuffs, then gently placed a hand on her shoulder. "And in the meantime, it makes for one hell of a club."

As Wander watched, he seated her quite comfortably in a gilded chair, one of those silly, little things you have in boudoirs. Expertly, he switched a cuff from her wrist to the carved armrest. "Can't have you running off," he said. "Undo all our hard work."

What if I already have? Panic seized her and she thought she really would be sick. *What if what I told Phobetor was enough for It to find this place, to see through the illusion?*

What if they suspect?

"You told me to run," she said. "I was going to."

Wander shook her deceptive head. "You went and got drunk, Madeline. That's dangerous, self-destructive behaviour."

"Are you counselling me now?" Madeline did her best to chuckle, but inside she was screaming. *They know and Wander has brought me here to make sure I don't escape.*

But all Wander did was smile and pat her arm. "You can rest here. Think things through." Madeline turned her head away and after a moment, Wander receded.

"More water?" Giselle was at her side now, offering her an ancient, china teacup. Madeline accepted it in her free hand and sipped the weird-tasting liquid, choosing not to wonder where it came from. Wondering how she could persuade Giselle to let her go.

"She was always completely frank, you know." Giselle took back the cup. "How she knew you, what was going on. She answered all my questions."

"What do you think she is?" Madeline asked, pitching her voice low. "Really."

"Did you ever hear of the Lady of Cao?" Giselle's reply was equally low. "It's a mummy they found in Peru, a great priest-queen. The wall paintings show her on a throne, drinking the blood of sacrifices." She lifted the cup and drank the rest of the water.

Madeline nodded, listening to the echoes of whatever was happening behind her, as Wander and Roscoe communed. Small, intimate sounds and the faint glissade of harp strings coalescing into something vast. As thought just beyond the walls was an infinite chorus of desire.

She felt, suddenly, tired. Which was ridiculous when she had been awake for barely an hour. But a haze ate at her thoughts and her head was heavy, like she was almost ready to sleep. And she could not sleep here. Of all things, she could not sleep!

She stiffened as Giselle lent closer. "When I found you asleep on the lounge where were you? What were you dreaming?"

"In the tunnels," she said "Of the Metro. I got lost getting back, that's why I was still... please, listen to me. I don't think I should be here, for Wander's sake. For your sake! I—" She shook her head sharply, against the vagueness.

"Just relax," Giselle whispered. "Everything's going to be fine. I may even forgive you."

The chorus sang in her ears. The chamber swam before her eyes. "The water," she gasped, struggling to focus on Giselle. "You put something in the water."

"Don't fight it." Giselle stroked her hair. "In a minute, everything will be just fine."

The light from the lamps seemed to flare up, then ooze across the stone like honey. She felt strangely buoyant, as though even her chains were made of silk. She sank back into the chair, promising herself that in a moment she would fight this, that she would not succumb to the languor, the drifting vapours and to Giselle's presence, that she had missed so much.

She rolled her head and Giselle was no longer wearing jeans. Somehow, she had changed clothes into something Madeline had never seen her wear, had never imagined she would. A corset of silver lace, the tatters of a gauzy skirt flowing over her hips. Around her neck was buckled a silver collar. Her eyes and skin were clear, and her sheer beauty was frightening.

Madeleine turned round in the chair and there was nothing tawdry, now, about Roscoe's creation. As night falls on a theme park, the lights kindle and it becomes a place of dreams. Now the LEDs bloomed seraphic shades, an Eden lit by the sword of fire. And Giselle gazed at her over a statue's shoulder, the statue embraced her, the perfect texture of the marble flesh against her bright skin. Her eyes were dilated and behind her, the columns *writhed*— Madeline shut her eyes and could still see them, feel them almost like a blade scraping across her skin. Feel their true shapes. Sense *stairs leading to other stairs, through archways to other paths, down colonnades to courtyards...*

Something huge and dark approaches. She feels it rumbling through the spirals surrounding them, feels the air thickening and recognises It. She will always recognise It, will spend the rest of her life fleeing from the moment when she took Its hand.

"It's coming," she said. But nobody responded. She turned further, found the stained-glass panel streaming crimson and blue, but the void at the centre was now filled with Giselle's face, her narrow shoulders, her high breasts. A sinful icon, her eyes were wide and filled with darkness, as dark liquid beaded on her forehead, on the smooth roundness of her upper arms.

Madeline swayed to her feet, the chain grating against her wrist. I'm not asleep, she thought, not really. But I dream nonetheless. "Fuck you," she said into the phantasmagoria. Then louder, "FUCK YOU!"

"Hush, Madeline." Wander spoke. "You really did leave me no choice."

Wander was in the tripod, of course. She all but hovered at the junction of coloured cords. They distributed her body's weight across her shoulders, beneath her arms and hips, lacing tight around her dead fish thighs.

Madeline walked right on over, dragging the chair behind her. It was her anchor, her link to reality. "These are some good drugs," she said, "I hope you know they aren't going to help."

"It's a just little oneirogen that most of our visitors use." Wander spun slowly, winding and unwinding. "It reveals the truth."

"Like I haven't heard that before," Madeline replied, "From junkies."

"You feel It now," said Wander, eyes green crescents, white skin twisting like wrung cloth as the cords pulled contrariwise. "Phobetor is circling. It knows you're here. You told me running wouldn't help, and you were right."

"That was when I thought that Phobetor was just a dream."

"My parent has come this close to me half a dozen times, over the past three years," said Wander. "The illusion works. All we need do is maintain our discipline, and that, my dear doctor, is what you lost."

Madeline looked down at her wrist, still chained. She looked at Giselle in the glass and took a step towards her. Then she saw Roscoe, moving in with what appeared to be a life-sized, marble phallus in his hands. She sat back down in the chair.

"Six weeks of therapy and you think you know it all," she muttered.

"About twenty years in bondage, I know quite a lot. And then there's everything before. I remember so much more, now. Knowledge I use to protect this place." And then the timbre of Wander's voice changed, sharply. "What the hell."

Madeline swung around, following the green gaze to the wall where Madeline supposed, they had entered. An utter impossibility was taking place.

It looked like a gigantic sunflower. Slowly unfurling as it heaved itself through what looked like a mere crack, it stood as tall as Roscoe on thick, articulated roots. The stem was as thick and ribbed as a human torso and it seemed to move by flexing. The flower head was massive, and Madeline stifled a scream, realising that instead of florets, the central disc was comprised of human teeth. Rings of cuspids and bicuspids, incisors gathered towards the centre and great, ropey molars extruding from the rim.

"A figment," said Wander, "It's just a figment but strong, so strong, I'll give you this, Madeline. I think It's found the entrance." She swung, agitated, then seemed to remember her own words. Collected herself. "But It can't be sure, now, can It?" She revolved slowly in her restraint. "This is meant to provoke a reaction. Don't give It one."

Madeline watched as the monstrosity lumbered across the floor, head turning blindly. Madeline lifted her hand above the back of the chair. "Wake up," she hissed to herself, then brought it down. The pain was jarring. But nothing changed.

The drug, she thought. I'm not really asleep, so I can't wake myself up. A floating terror seized her. "Wander, you *bitch*!"

But further words died in her throat, as a blunt snout of bluish grey nudged through the crack. As the mouth below opened, another gallery of teeth was revealed—but these were hooked, razor edges arranged in rows. Pin-head eyes sunk deep in grey and hairless skin. Fins scything for balance, as it teetered and finally straightened on muscular, hairy appendages.

It was, quite simply, a shark on legs. The point of merger was covered by fluorescent pink and orange board shorts.

"Call this a nightmare?" Wander muttered. "Ah, but you haven't finished yet, have you?"

The next thing to emerge was a small girl. She wore summer pyjamas, patterned with cats. Her hair was gold and curly, her skin a flushed apricot, suggestive of sunlight and laughter. She yawned and blinked about her curiously.

The shark turned on its stupid, flailing legs.

"Another figment," said Wander.

Madeline put her hand to her mouth as the child gazed up at the looming creature. But it was the sunflower, launching like a spring, that reached her first. It flexed its calyx and engulfed her. There was no sound, but chubby legs thrashed, and elbows and fist-shapes distorted the gathered petals.

Madeline whispered, "Are you sure?"

Blood drizzled down the stem.

"If it isn't," said Wander, "there's nothing I can do."

Gradually, the thrashing stopped. Madeline continued watching as next a golden-haired woman who was obviously the girl's mother wandered into the chamber, calling soundlessly. Her butchery by the shark was succeeded by that of a tall, gangly man whose skin was pale but hair a vivid red. As he was torn apart by both creatures, his eyes seemed to find the onlookers. He mouthed something silently, choked off in blood.

How long will this continue? Madeline thought, twisting the chain against her wrist. *Does Wander have any other relatives, or friends that aren't tied to something?*

"We have to leave," she told Wander.

"I'm showing you this for a reason, Madeline, so you won't take such chances again. Just stay calm."

Said the thing that just saw her human father devoured, without turning a hair. What kind of a psychological complex did *that* suggest? The foster family destroyed in effigy because the abused child didn't feel worthy of love. Wander said she remembered more, of what happened in the palace....

The palace that lay all around her in facsimile, a den of exquisite tortures and sick ecstasies. Knowing it was futile, Madeline shut her eyes again. On the inside of her lids, the columns resolved into forms as clear and golden as the dawning of the world.

When she opened her eyes, the crack had disgorged Farid Kateeb. He wore the same blue and red football jersey, and his skinny legs were bare. He looked confused, frightened, and very, very real. But Madeline did not react. She was a psychiatrist, after all, and understood all too well the game of bait and switch.

"One of yours?" Wander suggested.

He is real, Madeline thought. He has fallen asleep, as his parent said, in class or huddled up somewhere in the school grounds. Maybe he is even somewhere in the Metro. Him, I can wake. She gripped the base of the chair in both hands, struggling to pull her scattered thoughts together. "I thought he must belong to Roscoe," she said, casually, and the instant of distraction, as green eyes slipped from her to him, was enough. It had to be.

She grabbed the chair and ran towards her patient.

"Stop!" Roscoe ordered—for a big man, he was quick on his feet! "If you react, Phobetor will know."

"It already knows!" Madeline turned and faced that leather mask. In her drugged, waking dream, it was no mask, but a moving, monstrous face. But she had seen the mask and perhaps it was that, and the clasp of the handcuffs, that brought the words to her lips. They came from a memory, something read and repeated.

She cried out the safe word Wander had said they used, and Roscoe stopped.

With one huge hand, he gripped the leg of the chair. She was not free. But then, in his other, he produced a ridiculously tiny and delicate key.

Like an Apollo astronaut on the moon, when the cuff fell open, she leapt into the very midst of the monsters and seized Farid in her arms.

"She's here!" she cried, as the boy gripped her back—now more than ever, she knew he was real. "This isn't a real dream, she's *right here*!"

She heard no response from the tripod, even though she had just betrayed Wander within her hearing. The effort of escaping

Roscoe had left her light-headed, as if she were about to float away. She turned from the monsters to gage Wander's response, and oh, of course; all the winding paint trails and the bindings themselves were only ever part of Wander, her tatters extruding throughout the chamber. Twitching and flexing as slowly, she rose, hood forming, beak growing from her face.

The crack of the entrance was now a single, massive sheet of mould. A few skulls popped out, swept up by the growth, and rolled across the floor as the air shimmered.

"I'm sorry, Doctor." It was Farid, his face pressed into her shoulder. "I tried, but It got me. It made me walk." On either side, shark and sunflower drew themselves up, leaves curling, fins twisting for a killing blow.

Madeline raised her hand and slapped Farid hard across the face "Wake up," she ordered.

Farid looked at her, shocked. She shoved him hard, so he fell and hit the floor.

Nothing happened. He was still there. And then, she saw the mould reaching tendrils, tatters, across the stone towards him.

"Let him go," she addressed the mould. "Please."

She saw that the mould was blackening, and took this for a refusal. She had made no deal with Phobetor for Farid, only for Paris. She reached for the boy's arm and hauled him, whispering apologies, saying it would be all right, as step by step she retreated across the floor, back behind the barrier of statues and glass. "Please," she said, though lord knows there was no reason Wander should listen to her either. "Help him."

"He's dreaming," said Wander. There was wonder in her voice, as she realised how strong Farid was. "His body isn't here. He'll never make it past Phobetor," And now there was anguish. "I can't save him Madeline."

"But you have to." She felt tears in her eyes. "There has to be something—"

"But I can save you."

She gripped Farid. "We can't wake either. Thanks to your drug!"

"Madeline. Thanks to the drug, you can see Phobetor approaching in the dream. You know It affects the real, you've seen what It can do, to solid walls. But enough of this is still a dream, that if you go now, you may get past It. So long as I'm here to distract It." Wander's voice broke. "It won't be easy, but you can."

Madeline glanced back at the wall. Rot extended long tendrils into the ceiling, forcing them like roots beneath the buckling floor.

"Go," said Wander. "Run. Roscoe will lead you."

"And what, you'll stay?" Roscoe grated. "Keep It busy?"

"Don't worry," Madeline whispered to Farid. "I won't leave you. It will be all right."

"I won't do it," said Roscoe. "I will never leave you!"

"You must! And once you get back to the bar, get everyone in there out! In case…"

In case the ceiling in here collapses, thought Madeline, once Phobetor arrives. She said, "At least save Giselle."

As rot touched the discarded chair, Madeline turned away. She turned to Roscoe and the writhing thing with the woman's body, black beak and gleaming, serpent eyes. Clearly, he worshipped her: perhaps he always had. And there was a time when she, too, felt tatters wrapped around her and felt only safe.

Roscoe drew himself up, a statue of bronze. "I love you," he said to Wander, "But them I will save."

The tatters rose, winding around him, caressing him.

Madeline felt a sob in her throat. Felt sickness, then realised she did not know the difference.

Then she felt the brush of tatters against her cheek. "Dr Diomande? You tried to help me, even though I used you. You gave Roscoe and I these extra years. For that, I thank you."

"You opened my eyes," Madeline said, refusing to let either sob or sickness escape, "You made me see that a symbol could be so much more… a symbol." And then she knew. From the same place in her heart or mind that produced the safe word, she knew how Wander could save them all. And it was so simple, she almost wanted to laugh.

"Hurry now." The tatters agitated. "And remember, once the drug wears off, you still aren't safe."

"Not while Phobetor remains here. I know. I know." She reached up with one hand, gripped the tatters like the strings of a balloon. "But you could send It back."

"Madeline, I've grown stronger. But I'll never be that strong."

"Now listen to me, Wander. You built a symbol, a symbol of the Palace itself." She paused as before her, Roscoe forced Giselle towards the mould. The crevice spewed skulls, they would never make it. She forced conviction into her voice. "And what do we do with symbols? We use them to summon doors."

No longer a laugh, but a reptilian carolling came from Murmur's beak.

"You're telling me to open a door from the shallows beyond the deep!"

"You can do it," she said. "Symbolically, we're already there."

A shivering, creaking sound, perhaps from the frame, perhaps from Wander as she continued to change. "It's impossible!"

"For a human, maybe. Not for the Child of Phobetor."

"Even so. Even *if.* There's no waking from *there!*"

"Not for us, for *It!* Open a door and send It back!"

***

She was Wander Paxton, citizen of the world. Now she is more. She has always been more.

A step, a glissade, an obsequience, a flaring of wings; a single twist of black in an endless, white corridor. A step, a foot, a throne, a cracking of spine; centuries of agony, all for learning to speak! She slivers silvers into the sky and there are stars; It lets her build, just little things, then tears them down. She flies, she sings, she is poured into a mould, stretched across a grill derived from mortal dreams, again and again she is forced into forms she cannot control, helpless as she dances a gavotte across base terrors. It hunts with her, hooded and jessed on It's wrist It marries her, it buries her, it strokes her coils and hums to her, the lost princess found, the found princess lost.

It is so strange, thinking like this. But Madeline is right. Without even realising, she has bent all her efforts and those of her lover to this, channelled the fear and desire of all those who like Giselle, came to her for refuge, to create a symbol of the very thing she fled. But still, what is it but a bamboo picture? The imprint of a leaf.

Madeline, with her tourmaline skin and obsidian eyes. Who led Phobetor here, all for the sake of a child. Another clever little human, asking the impossible. For her, Wander will try.

This is more than she has ever attempted and to do it, she must find that inside her which is equivalent to Madeline's waves. She must accept the truth; she must look beneath the cowl.

She must do the work, accept that she—

That she—

That she *loved* It! How wretched and sick, that she wanted to please, to feel It's pleasure! And all that... love is abrading against her now, ready to claim her, ready to take her back. Nonetheless, she concentrates. Summons her memories, imaginings and hardest of all desires: she *feels* the foulness of it! Feels the tension of forty years straining against what she now does. But the door begins to form, materialising on the floor right in front of the crevice. It glows like ancient starlight. Like dawn on the first morning of the world. The stress is unbearable; she roars it with a hydra's throats. But does not let go.

She feels the walls of her sanctuary gape, the dream of ancient stone reduced to vapour. The seethe as a million tatters penetrate. Particles spurn vermiculite chaos assuming the shape of a cowl: beneath it, form constantly replaces form as It pours inside; a beast, a bird, a long serpent.

As It rises over the helpless forms of Roscoe and Giselle.

In that instant, she does the impossible. She conjures the Throne. An empty throne, in a palace left unguarded. It halts, in realisation of this unthinkable betrayal. It flattens Its hood—a defensive posture. But It does not take the bait.

You wouldn't dare.

One final time she laughs, then does the only thing she can. The only thing that will distract it. She lets herself go and falls, falls. Falls out of her body into an eternal dream.

The Child vanishes, the door closing behind It, and the lost Sovereign roars. Nothing else is important now, nothing else even registers as It spreads, diffusing Its rage like a wave across the whole, coralline terrain of dreaming Paris. The Child is home *now, walking the corridor of pure brightness, crossing the sanguine smoulder of the hall and climbing steps as old as sleep. Perhaps It even sits upon the throne. Is this possible? Perhaps It even now takes control of the defences, reaches out to allies, preparing to turn all against their rightful ruler. Rage and storm, inconceivable!*

And oh, Phobetor is weary of this littoral, its ephemera of memory and individuation. Such things are simply irritating to an entity that deals in archetypes. Worse still is the constant friction as It squeezes through these ridiculous limitations, coming at last to comprehend that the Child valued some individuations over others. That these frail beings formed their own links. Then forcing Its own peripheries into shapes that could speak. But such concepts are too meagre for It to really grasp and It has already forgotten the shapes upon the floor. It wants only to return.

And hasn't the Child been, after all, clever? Betrayal. War. There are archetypes for this situation. The possibilities are intriguing. Will the demi-dreams take her side? Will his sibling gods? Perhaps, after all, this is why It created a Child to begin with.

It coalesces deep in the tunnels, at Farid Kateeb's border, and passes through.

***

And Madeline wakes.

She lay contorted on cold stone, shaking uncontrollably. Her skin felt scorched, poisoned, and each muscle had been wrenched to breaking point. Her mouth was full of blood. But she was breathing, her heart was racing, and she remembered....

She was surrounded. Not just by Giselle and Roscoe: now there were others.

"You led It here," said Roscoe—dear God, he looked ghastly! He bent over her, hands empty and bleeding, blood trickling like tears from his eyes. "Why did you do that?"

She found a voice that rasped. "She didn't belong here. She never did."

They didn't touch her as somehow, she managed to sit up. She coughed and spat and saw.

The chamber walls had held, the roof was solid. But wreckage surrounded them on every side. Crumbled statues, shattered skulls, a talus of rubble washing across the floor. And at the centre lay Wander's body. Blasted white, eyes mere sockets and fingers, pubis bleeding black, upon a blackened bier. Her hair was in the rock now, strands crawling through limestone pressured to marble.

"There's a heartbeat," said Roscoe, but this could not possibly be true. Even though she felt it thudding inside her own head, a double drum.

There was no sign of Farid. The drug was gone from her system now, her every thought was hard and clear. But she prayed it was a good sign. That Farid had escaped, that he had woken in his own bed with rhymes coursing through his head and was not lost somewhere and screaming, screaming…

She turned, then, to face them. Giselle, her blonde hair ribboned with blood. Faces she did not know, all turned accusingly.

"She was hurting people," she says. "Hurting *you*. And It was never going to stop. This was the only way out, for any of us."

They closed in, the worshippers, unrelenting and deaf to all logic. Roscoe reached out with his big, strong hands and took her in a grip she could not break.

"You know how to dream," he said. "You flew with her like I never could. You are going to help me bring her *back*."

***

PARIS, 2019
And Madeline

Has not seen the sun for a very long time.

Has learned how to stretch and how to bend.

Cannot tell sleeping from waking, reality from dream. Only that the waves are rising, rising ever higher behind the walls.

But of late, something that resembles her brother has been speaking to her, from out of the dense, dark earth. He tells her what to do once the door to the palace is open—and the waves will break soon, very soon. What will happen then, ah, then! That is something which cannot be fathomed, even in the wildest of dreams.

ABOUT THE AUTHOR

KYLA LEE WARD is a graduate of the University of Technology, Sydney, who works in many modes, principally writing and acting. Reviewers have accused her of being "gothic and esoteric", "weird and exhilarating" and of having a "... real presence 'live' as she has too in these poems."

Her poetry has placed in the Rhyslings and garnered an Australian Shadows award. Her work up to 2019 is collected in two volumes from P'rea Press – *The Land of Bad Dreams* and *The Macabre Modern and Other Morbidities*. Her first short story collection, *This Attraction Now Open Till Late*, published in 2022 by Independent Legions.

A multiple Stoker finalist and nominee for Ditmar and Aurealis awards, her stories have otherwise appeared in Aurealis, Borderlands, and Shadowed Realms magazines, and in anthologies such as *Gods, Memes and Monsters: A Twenty-first Century Bestiary, The Lion and the Aardvark: Aesop's Modern Fables, The New Hero* Volume One and *Macabre: A Journey into Australia's Worst Fears*.

She is one third of Edwina Grey. The novel *Prismatic* (Lothian 2006) was penned with her partner David Carroll and mutual friend Evan Paliatseas, but somehow won an Aurealis Award for Best Horror.

Her acting career has been long and varied. If you know where to look, she can be spotted in *The Artful Dodger* and *Mad Max: Fury Road*. She is a regular performer with James Adams Historic Enterprises, bringing the delights of medieval combat and culture to schoolchildren, and has been your *Guide to Deadhouse: Tales of Sydney Morgue* (Blancmange Productions) for four seasons thus far. Composing the occasional script, her short film, 'Bad Reception', screened at the Third International Vampire Film Festival and she was a member of the Theatre of Blood repertory 98 company, which produced her work alongside classic plays of the Grand Guignol.

A LARPer and role-player, she was a freelance writer for the White Wolf Gaming Studio as well as contributing to many magazines. Active in fandom since the '90s (when she and David edited the horror 'zine Tabula Rasa), her involvement culminated in programming the horror stream for Aussiecon 4 (the 68th Worldcon) in 2010. She has travelled widely, seen much that is dark and strange, and now hosts regular true crime and ghost tours in her hometown. A practicing occultist, she likes raptors, sword play and the Hellfire Club. To see some very strange things, including filmed performances, try HTTP://WWW.KYLAWARD.COM

WWW.INDEPENDENTLEGIONS.COM

AVAILABLE BOOKS IN ENGLISH

THE SIXTH SENTINEL
by Alessandro Manzetti & Stefano Fantelli
Grahic Novel – Paperback Edition
December 2023

TEXTURE OF SILENCE
by Eugen Bacon & Steve Simpson
Prose Poetry Collection – Paperback Edition
December 2023

DEMONS
by John Shirley
Novel – Paperback Edition
September 2023

THE KEEPER OF CHERNOBYL
by Alessandro Manzetti
Novella – Paperback and eBook Edition
July 2023

STRANGE TALES OF TERROR
Edited by Eugene Johnson
Anthology – Hardcover Edition
December 2022

THE ANA LOG AND OTHER ANOMALIES
by Michael Gray Baughan
Collection – Paperback and eBook Edition
November 2022

MOBIUS LYRICS
by Angela Yuriko Smith and Maxwell I. Gold
Poetry Collection – Paperback and eBook Edition
October 2022

THIS ATTRACTION NOW COMING TILL LATE
by Kyla Lee Ward
Collection – Paperback and eBook Edition
September 2022

KRAKEN INFERNO
by Alessandro Manzetti and Stefano Cardoselli
Graphic Novel – Paperback Edition
April 2022

DANCING WITH MARIA'S GHOST
by Alessandro Manzetti i
Poetry Collection– Paperback and eBook Edition
December 2021

THE INHABITANT OF THE LAKE
by Alessandro Manzetti and Stefano Cardoselli
Graphic Novel – Paperback Edition
December 2021

BLACK MOUNTAIN
by Simon Bestwick
Novel – Paperback and eBook Edition
November 2021

APACHE WITCH
by Joe R. Lansdale
Poetry Collection – Hardcover Edition
September 2021

THE FEVERISH STARS
by John Shirley
Collection – Paperback and eBook Edition
March 2021

HER LIFE MATTERS
by Alessandro Manzetti and Stefano Cardoselli
Graphic Novel – Paperback Edition
December 2020

UMBRIA
by Santiago Eximeno
Collection – Paperback and eBook Edition
December 2020

LOST TRIBE
by Gene O'Neill
Novel – Paperback and eBook Edition
October 2020

SHILOH
by Philip Fracassi
Novella – Paperback and eBook Edition
October 2020

WHITECHAPEL RHAPSODY
by Alessandro Manzetti
Poetry Collection – Paperback and eBook Edition
October 2020

RED DENNIS
by Eric Shapiro
Novel – Paperback and eBook Edition
March 2020

THE DEMETER DIARIES
by Marge Simon and Bryan D. Dietrich
Prose/Poetry Collection – Paperback and eBook Edition
October 2019

THE MAN WHO ESCAPED THIS STORY AND OTHER STORIES
by Cody Goodfellow
Collection – Paperback and eBook Edition
September 2019

CROTA
by Owl Goingback
Novel – Hardcover, Paperback and eBook Edition
July 2019

DARK CARNIVAL
by Joanna Parypinski
Novel – Paperback and eBook Edition
June 2019

CALCUTTA HORROR
by Alessandro Manzetti & Stefano Cardoselli
Graphic Novel – Paperback and eBook Edition
May 2019

COYOTE RAGE
by Owl Goingback
Novel – Paperback and eBook Edition
February 2019

APARTMENT SEVEN
by Greg F. Gifune
Novella – Paperback and eBook Edition
Juanuary 2019

FEARFUL SYMMETRIES
by Thomas F. Monteleone
Collection – Paperback and eBook Edition
January 2019

DARK MARY
by Paolo Di Orazio
Novel – Paperback and eBook Edition
December 2018

TRIBAL SCREAMS
by Owl Goingback
Collection – Paperback and eBook Edition
October 2018

MONSTERS OF ANY KIND
Edited by Alessandro Manzetti & Daniele Bonfanti
Anthology – Paperback and eBook Edition
September 2018

ARTIFACTS
by Bruce Boston
Poetry Collection– Paperback and eBook Edition
July 2018

KNOWING WHEN TO DIE
by Mort Castle
Collection– Paperback and eBook Edition
June 2018

NARAKA
by Alessandro Manzetti
Novel– Paperback and eBook Edition
May 2018

A WINTER SLEEP
by Greg F. Gifune
Novel– Paperback and eBook Edition
April 2018

SPREE AND OTHER STORIES
by Lucy Taylor
Collection – Paperback and eBook Edition
February 2018

THE LIVING AND THE DEAD
by Greg F. Gifune
Novel – Paperback and eBook Edition
December 2017

TALKING IN THE DARK
by Dennis Etchison
Collection – eBook Edition
December 2017

THE BEAUTY OF DEATH 2 – DEATH BY WATER
edited by Alessandro Manzetti & Jodi Renee Lester
Anthology – Paperback and eBook Edition
November 2017

DREAMS THE RAGMAN
by Greg F. Gifune
Novella – Paperback and eBook Edition
November 2017

CHILDREN OF NO ONE
by Nicole Cushing
Novella – Paperback and eBook Edition
October 2017

THE RAIN DANCERS
by Greg F. Gifune
Novella – Paperback and eBook Edition
September 2017

THE WISH MECHANICS
by Daniel Braum
Collection – Paperback and eBook Edition
July 2017

THE ONE THAT COMES BEFORE
by Livia Llewellyn
Novella – Paperback and eBook Edition
May 2017

SELECTED STORIES
by Nate Southard
Collection – Paperback and eBook Edition
March 2017

THE CARP-FACED BOY AND OTHER TALES
by Thersa Matsuura
Collection – Paperback and eBook Edition
February 2017

DOCTOR BRITE
by Poppy Z. Brite
Collection – eBook Edition
December 2016

**ALL AMERICAN HORROR OF THE 21ST CENTURY: THE FIRST
DECADE**
edited by Mort Castle
Anthology – Paperback and eBook Edition
November 2016

BENEATH THE NIGHT
by Greg Gifune
Novel – Paperback and eBook Edition
October 2016

THE HORROR SHOW
by Poppy Z. Brite
Collection – eBook Edition
August 2016

THE BEAUTY OF DEATH VOL. 1
Edited by Alessandro Manzetti
Anthology – eBook Edition
July 2016

SELECTED STORIES
by Edward Lee
Collection – eBook Edition
July 2016

USED STORIES
by Poppy Z. Brite
Collection – eBook Edition
June 2016

THE USHERS
by Edward Lee
Collection – eBook Edition
May 2016

THE CRYSTAL EMPIRE
by Poppy Z. Brite
Novella – eBook Edition
April 2016

SONGS FOR THE LOST
by Alexander Zelenyj
Collection – eBook Edition
April 2016

SELECTED STORIES
by Poppy Z. Brite
Collection – eBook Edition
February 2016

THE HITCHHIKING EFFECT
by Gene O'Neill
Collection – eBook Edition
February 2016

INDEPENDENT LEGIONS PUBLISHING
Via Virgilio, 10 – TRIESTE (ITALY)
+39 040 9776602
www.independentlegions.com
independent.legions@aol.com

www.ingramcontent.com/pod-product-compliance
Lightning Source LLC
Chambersburg PA
CBHW031438150726
47989CB00002B/980